THE MYSTERY OF THE DRAKON MINES

Vedanth S. Reddy

Made with ♥ on the Notion Press Platform
www.notionpress.com

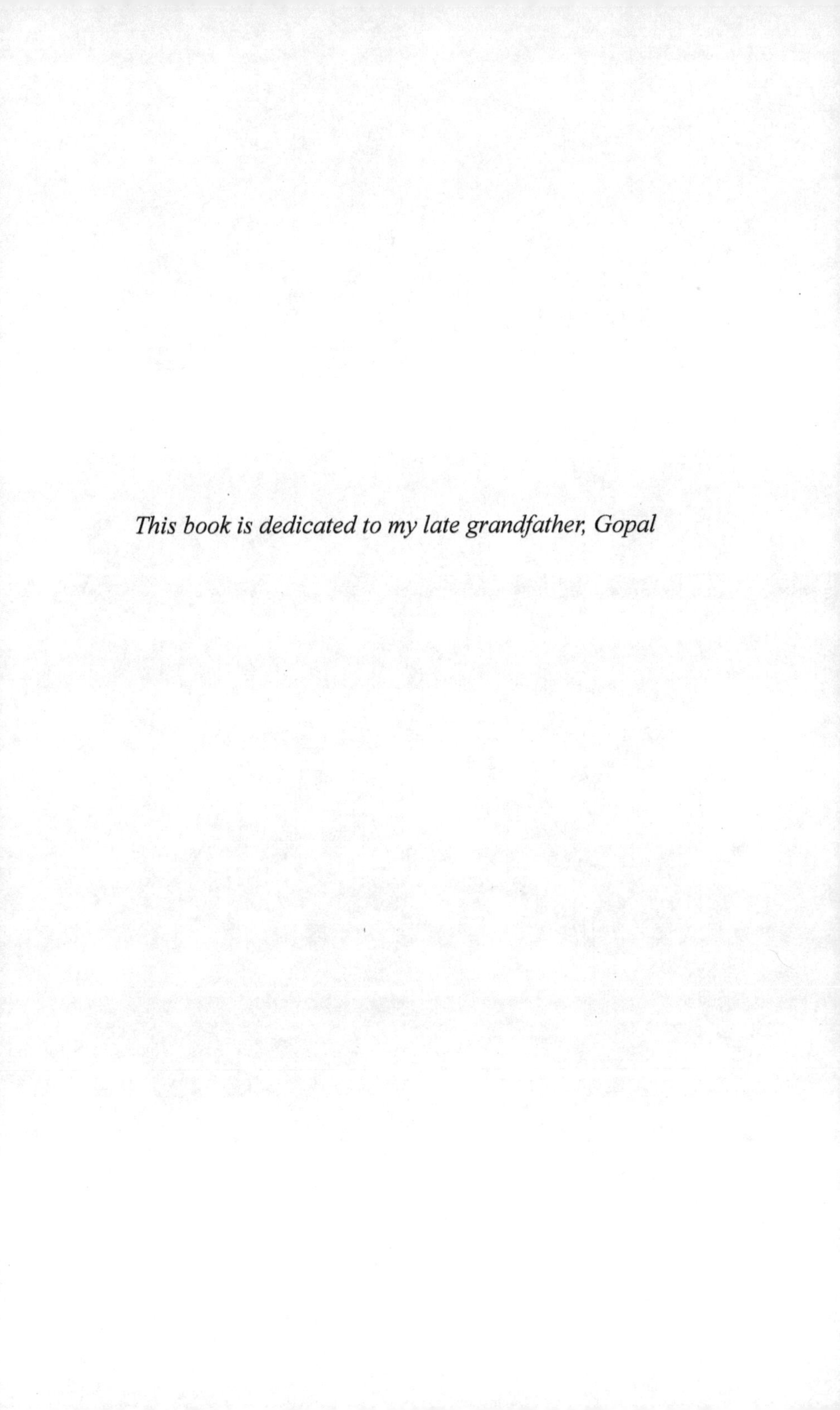

This book is dedicated to my late grandfather, Gopal

CONTENTS

THE MYSTERY OF THE DRAKON MINES

THE GERMAN CONNECTION

Chapter 1

My entire life changed in one night. It all began on March 8, 2021, and my life could not be more different now. But before I tell you the whole story, let me give you a brief introduction. My name is Leo Schmidt, and I live in Vancouver with my mom and dad. I'm in my second year at Welser University. I barely talk to anyone, except for Aaliyah and James. Ever since I was a kid, I was constantly bullied for being an introvert but these two pals of mine always had my back.

My dream was to just be rich. I had no idea how, but I just wanted to be rich. I was fed up with living in that junkyard my mom called a house -- it had two rooms and an attic that couldn't be opened. Well, that's basically my life but as I told you, everything changed that night. It all started a few days before that. I woke up at 6 am and got ready. I decided to wear my new sweater which my mom had gifted on my birthday. I drank my morning coffee and walked to Aaliyah's house down the road. I waited for her to get ready, and we walked until the bus stop. On the bus to university, she was quiet throughout the whole journey and did not even comment on my new sweater. We reached campus and went to the cafeteria to grab breakfast.

"What's up? You look bitter," I said.

"Finally, you asked me. I just miss my dad," she smiled and replied.

Aaliyah's dad was a cop and a well-respected one. One day, when he was walking back with Aaliyah from dinner, a robber jumped them and asked for all their money. Aaliyah's father co-operated but when he tried to pull out his gun, the robber shot him dead in front of Aaliyah and ran away. Aaliyah was extremely scared, and many people rushed to the spot, but they could not catch the robber. The police investigated the matter and found the robber, but the damage done to Aaliyah was severe. She was eight years old then and was raised by her mother ever since. She tries to forget this memory, but it scares her when she thinks of it.

"I know it's really hard to lose your father, but would he want to see you unhappy," I said.

"I don't know, forget that we talked about this and let's get to class." Aaliyah said.

At that exact moment, James arrived. He is a very rambunctious kid and always manages to get into trouble. "Hey, what you guys talking about?" he asked.

"Nothing let's get to class," Aaliyah replied.

I knew she did not want James to know that she was unhappy due to her father's death, as he would make a big deal out of it. James cares for her a lot and it always hurts him when she is unhappy even in the slightest.

All three of us had economics class. We immediately noticed something peculiar. Our usual teacher was not there, instead we saw another person. He looked like he was in his mid-thirties, he wore round glasses and a maroon suit. In short, he was dressed like a gentleman. We assumed he was a substitute teacher and sat down. He informed all of us that the economics teacher was not present at the moment, and he would be teaching us history today. Everyone was okay with that, but we had no interest in the subject. To my surprise, he showed us a map. He spoke for almost an hour and gave me an awkward smile before walking out of the room. I felt a bit weird, and I had no clue why he smiled at me. We finished our remaining classes and were heading back home. We saw the man again and he kept looking at me. He approached the three of us.

"You must be Leo Schmidt, Aaliyah Thomas and James Anderson." he said.

I was extremely frightened. How did this man, whom I'd never seen in my life, knew my name. "Yes, and how do you know our names Sir?" I asked.

The man smiled. 'My name is Julius, and if you guys are okay to grab a cup of coffee, I can explain everything.'

"There is a coffee shop nearby. Wanna take a walk?" James asked. Julius laughed. "That place is pretty cheap. Why don't you guys sit in my car, and we can go to Malrow's Café?"

Malrow's Café is the most expensive coffee shop in all of Vancouver and none of us could afford it. We walked up to his car, and he insisted that I sit in front. It was a one-hour drive from the university, so Aaliyah and James were talking with each other, but I was stuck in the front seat with Julius.

"So, Leo, what do you know about your family's history?" Julius asked.

"My grandparents were originally from Germany, but they moved to Canada many years ago for some reason," I said.

"I see," he said and chuckled.

There was an awkward silence between us while Aaliyah and James kept talking and laughing.

We finally reached the place and there was already a table reserved for us. The three of us ordered for a latte I usually like black coffee, but I wanted to try this for a change. Julius told the waiter he would take the usual.

The waiter replied, 'Yes sir,' and walked away. At that exact moment we knew something was wrong.

"I am going to get straight to the point. Do you know who your grandfather was, Leo?" Julius asked.

"Umm I don't think so, but why are you asking me all of this?" I replied.

Julius got really angry. 'Your grandfather's name is Jacob Weiser, and he stumbled upon a lost treasure in the Drakon Mines. We believe you have his map, and we would like to offer you a chance to join us on the quest to find the treasure,' he said.

I was confused and had no clue what to say. I never knew my

grandfather, and the story of the mines was a made-up one my mom would tell me as a kid.

"The mines are a bunch of crap; it is just a myth. Why would I have a map! And Jacob Weiser is not my grandfather. My grandfather died of a heart attack in Germany, and my grandma and my dad moved to Canada after. I believe you have the wrong person -- and, what do you mean by 'we'?" I asked the man, confused.

The coffee arrived and the four of us took a sip. It was the best coffee I have had till date.

"Look, we are giving you a week's time. If you are interested, call this number. But if we do not get a response, you and your friends will face serious consequences," Julius said.

He handed us a card with a number on it. He paid the bill and walked away. The three of us were extremely scared.

"What if this man is not joking and if your grandfather actually found the treasure?" James asked.

"That's literally impossible. If he found the treasure, why would me and my family be so poor!" I said.

"It's really late guys, can we go back to our homes and discuss about this tomorrow?" Aaliyah asked. We agreed and caught the bus. I reached home very late. My mom was waiting for me in the living room. "We were extremely worried about you, why didn't you pick up our calls? Where were you?" she asked.

"I was at a party, and it got late, I am sorry." I said. She just walked away disappointed as I went to my room. It was a holiday the next day, so I was not worried about college. I could not sleep all night and kept thinking about what the man said. Could my grandfather really be Jacob Weiser?

I woke up the next morning and made my usual black coffee. My father was sitting at the table. I asked him, "Who is my grandfather?"

"Why do you want to know about him?" he asked.

"Well, I am really curious about our family's history." I said.

"He was a terrible man and there is nothing to talk about him." he said.

"Please dad, I want to know who my grandad is." I asked.

"Your grandfather's name was Jacob Weiser, and he was a pathetic father to me. He left his wife and son alone for a long time and went in search of gold. But he never returned and was found dead. I was 15 years old at that time and my mom had no choice but to leave the country with me and we moved to Canada. We had to change our last name because your grandma felt it was a curse. We didn't have a single penny, but we did odd jobs and made a living somehow." My father said.

"But I thought he died of a heart attack?" I asked.

"Your mom and I did not know what to tell you when you were little, so we lied," he said.

I was shocked at hearing this. "Did he find the gold?" I asked.

My father laughed loudly. "If he found it, he wouldn't be found dead in some desert, and we wouldn't be so poor. Your grandfather was a madman and imagined all the gold." he said.

"Do you know anything about the treasure?" I asked.

"It doesn't exist. But from what your grandmother told me, it was located in some mine in Spain. Anyways, it's time for me to get to work, you have a great day," he said.

I took a quick shower and remembered I had to meet Aaliyah and James to discuss the situation regarding Julius. I called them to the park. I cycled and was the first one to reach. As usual, both of them came together, thirty minutes late. I did not bother because I was extremely worried. We sat together and began the meeting, if that is what we could call it.

"So, was this man lying, or is your grandfather really Jacob?" Aaliyah asked.

"It's all true, but from what my father told me, there is no gold, and my grandfather was a mad man," I said.

James interrupted. "What if your father is not sure and it really exists?" He asked.

"Why would his father lie?" Aaliyah said.

I smiled at Aaliyah. "There's only one way to know but it's impossible." I said.

THE ATTIC
Chapter 2

Aaliyah and James stayed over. We waited for my parents to fall asleep. I went to the dining area and dragged a chair to my room without making any noise. I stood on top of it and opened the attic door. As soon as I did, a huge pile of dust fell on my face. I wiped it off and climbed up to the attic. The whole room was dark, and I could not see anything. I remembered I had a torch in my room under the bed, so I told James and Aaliyah to get it. He proceeded to do so and the both of them climbed up to the attic and turned it on. The whole room was filled with carton boxes and various household items. We found the lights and turned them on. Surprisingly, they were working.

"Let's open all the boxes and maybe if we are lucky, we can find your grandpa's belongings?" James said.

We searched a ton of boxes but none of them had the name Jacob Weiser, there were boxes with my name, my parent's name and my uncle's name. We looked at all the boxes but there was one left which had the name of Jeremiah Schmidt.

"Who is this guy, Leo?" Aaliyah asked.

'I have no clue; I don't know anyone by this name." I said.

"Well, who gives a shit, can we just open this?" James asked.

I took out my pocketknife and used it to open the box. Inside, we saw an envelope, compass, backpack, knives, and a weird-shaped box that was locked. James yelled. "Holy crap, I think this belongs to your grandpa!"

I told him to shut up as he was making too much noise. I couldn't understand why my grandpa's belongings were in a box under Jeremiah Schmidt's name. The compass was in perfect condition, but the backpack was torn apart. I opened the backpack, and we saw a gun and a notebook.

"Holy shit!" Aaliyah exclaimed.

"I've always wanted to hold a gun!" James said.

He took it from the backpack and checked if it was loaded – luckily, it wasn't. I had so many questions at that moment. "Why was James so interested in guns? I scolded him and put it back in the backpack. I got the notebook out and proceeded to flip through the pages. Most of it was about my grandfather's hunt for treasure and some were weird texts which looked like some sort of ancient language. I wondered how my grandfather wrote this ancient language and proceeded to read his notes. I checked out the knives and put it back as they were extremely sharp.

There was an envelope in the bag too, which was sealed. It was written by Jacob Weiser. We opened it and read the letter:

"Dear son,

I know I haven't been a great father to you, but I always want you to be happy. I know I owe you an explanation, I went missing for a really long time but trust me, it was worth it.

I was once visited by a young man who was saying he needed help. He took me to his village, and I treated all the people who needed help but in return they gave me a map to a place, they told me to collect my reward from here. I did not bother with it at first, but when I saw the map, I noticed it pointed to the lost Drakon mines, a famous myth among Germans. I decided to go back to visit the young man, but to my surprise, the village did not exist! It felt like I went to an imaginary place, I could not find any trace of it.

I gathered more information about the treasure and felt God had given me a path to become rich by giving me a direct map. I left you and your mother behind and set out on my journey. I travelled to many places and met many people, made a few friends and even a few enemies. But before I could fulfil my dreams, I was captured by others who are behind this gold. If you are reading this letter, I am dead. My good friend, Julia Fraiser, has escaped from this wretched place with my belongings and she must have delivered them to you. All I wish to tell you is that the map is in the box and if you meet Julia, she will give you the key to open this box. I hope you find this gold.

Yours lovingly,
Jacob Weiser."

Reading my grandfather's words and tragic story made me sad. "Wait, that means your father never read this letter," Aaliyah said. I nodded, sighing.

"So how do we meet this Julia, isn't she probably dead?" James asked.

We surfed the internet for a really long time, looking for Julia. We finally found her mentioned in a really old article 13 years ago. It said that she was a historian and went in search of treasure with a doctor (my grandfather!). We found her official website and saw that she was currently living in Toronto. Her phone number was displayed on the bottom. I was glad she lived nearby and gave her a call. Someone picked up.

"Who is this?" the voice said.

"Uh, I'm Leo Schmidt, am I talking to Julia Fraser?" I asked.

"I am her assistant. She is busy at the moment; can we call you later?" she said.

"Wait don't cut the call, tell her my grandfather is Jacob Weiser and I need the key!" I said.

She put the call on hold, and minutes later, someone else spoke. "My name is Julia. Come to Toronto within 24 hours," she said.

She cut the call without any explanation, and we had no option but to go there now. I had no idea what to do. I could either ditch my college education and hunt for this treasure or work hard and get an ordinary job with a low salary. Being the idiot I am, I chose the treasure without knowing I had just waged a war with multiple people. I packed my grandfather's things, and we locked the attic door. The three of us went to sleep and I felt my whole life had taken a new turn.

JACOB WEISER'S JOURNAL
Chapter 3

My name is Jacob Weiser, and I am a hardworking, honest man. I am a doctor in a well-reputed hospital and earn enough money for my needs. I have a son named Thomas Weiser and my beautiful wife Lucia Weiser. I am currently 27 years old. I am writing this for the information of anyone who might read my story and learn the truth of my death.

One day, a shabby looking man entered my office, crying for help. A lot of people in his village had fallen ill due to an infection, and they needed a cure immediately. I agreed and he showed me the way to his village outside Rottenburg, where I am from.

It turned out that the people were infected by contaminated water, and I was able to treat them all. I did not take any money from them as I knew they could not afford much; but curiously, the man who had first approached me gave me a rolled-up piece of paper. Before I could open it, the man stopped me and told me to go back home and collect the reward.

Back in Rottenburg, I went back to the hospital and finished my work. When I went back home and went up to my room, I remembered the paper and opened it. At first glance it looked like a map of their village, but after observing it very carefully, I realised it was the map to the lost Drakon mines.

I couldn't believe it -- the treasure of the lost Drakon mines was a myth! There was a prophecy that said only the worthy could claim the gold. But this couldn't be -- I thought the man was joking with me and put it in my drawer. But for the next few weeks, my mind was completely occupied with this map. I finally decided to open the drawer and observe the map again. I visited tens of libraries to find out more about it, but only one book mentioned it. According to the book, there were many myths and legends around the world about the treasure, but none were reliable. There was one thing that all the stories mentioned, though: the only way to find the treasure was to find the map first, which had been lost to time.

I felt as though God was giving me a sign to be the one to find this treasure. I had more questions and decided to visit the man in the village. But when I followed the road, to my surprise, I could not find the place. It all felt like a dream. There was not a single trace of the houses and roads, or the clinic where I treated the patients. I did not know where else to look for answers.

I remembered a historian located in this city, who was known for discovering an ancient monument in South America. I found out where she lived and sent her a letter explaining my situation. At first, I got no reply from her, so I had given up on this treasure. After a few weeks, I had got a letter from one Julia Fraiser. She did not believe I had the map and asked me to meet her in her office. When she saw it, she was shocked.

She verified the map's authenticity -- we actually had a chance of finding the treasure. She told me to join her on this quest, but I was not ready to give her an answer yet. I told her I would get back to her the next day. That night, I thought for a really long time. Finally, I decided to join her and packed my bags. I did the most foolish thing and left my family without any explanation.

The next day, Julia made some time to study the map. Our first stop was Switzerland. Before leaving, she warned me that the journey would be dangerous and that we may not return. I was so deeply absorbed in finding this treasure that ignored everything else, even though I knew it was wrong.

It took us a week to reach Switzerland by boat. Julia had a few friends there, who were waiting for us. They took us to a nearby hotel and we showed them the map. They were stunned and asked me how I got it.

With their help, we learned that our quest would begin in Brazil.

They helped us book a flight and we were off the next day. But when we reached, we realised our journey was just beginning. We could not understand the rest of the map as it was written in an unidentifiable language.

Julia and I understood only English and German, so it was difficult to communicate with the locals. We assumed they would know at least something about the mines, but we had no luck.

After a lot of enquiring, we finally met a man who told us to visit the Santos library, as it may have what we were looking for. We did what the man told us. The library had only one book on the mines, and it was in Portuguese. We flipped through the pages and found multiple sketches, maps and notes, but they were useless as we couldn't understand it. We had to find a trustworthy translator. Luckily, Julia had a friend in Greece, named Michelle, who could help us. She wrote to her asking for her expertise.

While Julia and I waited for a reply, we did a lot of sightseeing and the both of us became really good friends. I was missing my family, but I could not do anything about it now. One fine afternoon, Julia received a package – the translation!

We came to know that there were four locations to be visited before getting our hands on this treasure. At each location was a clue to the puzzle, and here in Rio, we found out that we had to go to Belarus next. We saw various inscriptions and multiple sketches in the book. About the markings and notes, Michelle said they were written in a language that seemed a mix of Sanskrit, Spanish, French, Italian and other European tongues.

I was disappointed that we had such a long journey ahead of us before reaching the gold. When we reached Brest, we had to begin our search for the next clue. The city was beautiful and the food there was delicious. We decided to use our previous idea and searched every single library in the town, with no results. We asked the locals about it too, in vain. Local historians didn't seem to know anything either, except one. There was only one historian in the whole city who dealt with treasures. Everyone claimed that he was a mad man who left his wife because of his passion for treasures. Was he the one we were looking for?

His house looked pretty small from the outside and we knocked on the door. An old man opened the door and asked us who we were. We explained everything to him and asked if he knew about this treasure. To our surprise, he was happy when we told him this. He had been looking for this treasure for a long time as well, as it was connected to Belarus. However, he had not known about the other locations, so he had given up hope. We told him about the book, and he asked us if he could see it.

When we handed it to him, we witnessed a miracle. He was able to read all the markings written in the ancient text, which sounded a little like German. He said the map only marked Belarus and Brazil, and to find the next location, we would need to visit the Holy Mary Church in Brest. He knew about it and told us that it was written by a woman named Mary Thompson.

The historian couldn't help us anymore. Eventually, we found out about a Holy Mary Church, but it was closed for many years. We went there intending to break in, but the door was surprisingly open. The whole place was covered with cobwebs and dust -- it had probably not been cleaned in over a decade. We searched the whole church for any clue. We finally spotted a small keyhole in the crucifix symbol behind the pulpit. It was extremely small and very difficult to notice. So, finding the key was the next step.

Upon searching the place further, we found a really small room, but it was locked. We broke the door down and managed to find the key in one of the drawers.

When we went back to the pulpit, we turned the key and my god! A secret passageway opened below us. There was a flight of stairs leading down, but it was dark. Julia sparked her lighter and we walked. The passageway led to a strange map room. The walls were covered with portraits of various sailors and pirates. We saw a lot of books about the mines and took everything we could. We turned to the huge map on the wall. Apart from Brazil and Belarus, it showed the third location as the Atacama Desert. We were shocked -- what kind of clue could be found in a desert?

The next day, we picked up a telephone directory, looking for

Mary Thompson. We narrowed our search down to only three people -- Michael Thompson, Amanda Thompson, and Marlin Thompson. There was no Mary Thompson, but we assumed she was dead. One of these three people had to be her kin. We visited Amanda and Marlin, both of whom did not know any Mary Thompson.

We then went to Michael's house. Luckily, we found out his grandmother was Mary Thompson. We spoke with him for a while, and he told us that his grandmother was a lunatic. He explained that several years ago, she found out about these mines and devoted herself to it, ignoring her family. She searched for the treasure everywhere, but she managed to get to only to the first three locations and died somewhere in the Atacama Desert.

Before that, however, she wrote a book that was still in a library in Rio. She converted the family church into a research headquarters. She left all these clues so that others could find the treasure. Michael suddenly got very worked up and agitated and told us to leave.

We were disappointed about not finding out more about the treasure, but at least now we knew who Mary Thompson was. We decided to not waste any more time and arranged our travel to Atacama. It was a 23-hour flight to Chile, so Julia and I spoke for a really long time. I found out that Julia has a son and husband, who died in a car crash four years ago. She was devastated. I was really missing my family too and felt like hugging my son at that moment.

We landed in Calama, the closest city to the Atacama Desert. We found out about the Escondida copper-gold-silver mines, but we were pretty sure these weren't the lost Drakon mines. We assumed there was a second mine located in the desert. It was very difficult finding the place, though – we wandered the desert for weeks. We even found the Escondida mines, but they were owned by the government, so we did not bother going inside. Defeated, we went back to the city.

One day, at our hotel, we were greeted by an elderly man. He wanted to talk to us about something – he was looking for the treasure too! He knew that we had a map with us and asked to see it. He told us that if he saw the map properly, he could take us to the next clue. We did not believe this man and did not give him the map. He told us that there would be serious consequences to our actions and walked out of the motel.

When we left our room that evening, we were shocked to see that we were surrounded by seven men with guns. The same elderly man from before came towards us. He told us that that he killed all the staff, and that he would kill us too. We asked him what he wanted from us, and we couldn't believe his reply. His name was Diego Carlos, and he was a professor at a university. He had been looking for the treasure for twenty-five years but could never get his hands on the map with the final location. He had his men stationed across the city, which is how he found out about us.

He had us at gun-point – there was no way to escape. We had to give him the map. We were shocked again when he was able to read the strange markings. He said he finally knew where to go, but he would need our help.

The next day, we went into the desert together. We had no idea where he was taking us, but we were extremely scared as the three of them had loaded guns. It was a really long and extremely bumpy drive. He took us to some sort of cave, and we had to walk from there. I felt Diego was dangerous and was planning on killing us. We went inside the depths of the cave until we came upon a large boulder covered in the same ancient writing.

Diego read out the words and my God! The rocks started shaking and the whole cave began falling apart. Only Julia and I made it out alive. We were extremely frightened but glad those men were dead.

We took Diego's jeep and started driving back, but it was getting late, so we decided to stop and catch some sleep. Suddenly, in the middle of the night, we were woken up by a bright blue light. It was coming towards us. At first glance it looked like an animal, but as it got closer, we saw it was actually Diego! We had no idea what had happened to him, but we didn't wait to find out. We tried getting away from him, but he unleashed a lightning bolt at us, and the car crashed.

Julia was severely injured, and Diego was approaching us. I carried Julia in my arms and started running, but he was extremely fast and hit me with a lightning bolt. I told Julia to run away. I tried to fight him, but he had superhuman powers. He injured me severely and was almost about to kill me, when he suddenly stopped. He started glowing brighter and it looked like he was about to explode.

I ran away with Julia just as he exploded in a giant beam of light. We were in shock. I noticed that I was bleeding and had no chance of survival.

This is Julia. I am completing Jacob's diary after his tragic and violent death. He was a brave man who saved me, and he really loved his family. With his dying breath, he told me to forget about the treasure. He wanted his belongings returned to his wife and son, along with a letter, which I will do as soon as possible. He was a hero.

THE HISTORIAN

Chapter 4

Toronto was five hours away from Vancouver by flight.

James suggested that we drive, as we were broke, and I reminded him that it was a forty-one-hour journey from Vancouver. We finally booked the tickets, and luckily there was a flight in three hours. We went back to our homes, and we told our parents that we were going to Toronto for a college trip. We packed our bags and left the guns and knives in the attic.

We went to the airport and still had an hour left for our flight, so we waited at a restaurant.

"What if this Julia is some crazy lady and she's the one who killed your grandfather?" James said.

"My grandfather literally told us to trust her in that letter," I replied.

We argued for a while about his conspiracy theories regarding Julia. We boarded our flight and had the best time. We did the most amazing thing ever -- sleep! We woke up just as we landed in Toronto. Not knowing where to go and what to do, we called Julia and informed her that we'd reached. She told us to meet her at her house and sent the location through text. But first, we decided to mess around for a bit and went to an ice cream parlour. I had the bubble gum flavour.

We realised a lot of time had passed by, so we went to Julia's house.

We had read my grandfather's journal, so we knew she was rich. But we were shocked seeing her house. It was massive and guarded by a lot of security. We approached the main gate and were stopped by the guards. We had to show our faces in the camera and were allowed inside. As soon as we entered, we saw a huge garden and a swimming pool. James was getting bad vibes from the surrounding and tried to stop us from entering the house, but we went ahead. We rang the doorbell and a lady in a wheelchair welcomed us. She didn't say anything and just pointed towards a room. We followed the directions and went in. She came in too and locked the door, which creeped us out.

"So which one of you is Jacob's grandson." she asked.

"It's me, ma'am." I said.

She smiled. "How did you find out about me and who told you that I knew Jacob?"

"We read his journal and letter. We never knew my grandfather was a treasure hunter until this week. Aaliyah, my friend, read about you on the internet." I replied.

She sighed with disappointment. "So, your dad never read the letter, and it was just kept like that," she said. I nodded.

"What happened after my grandfather died?" I asked.

"Your grandfather was a great man. He was definitely stupid to leave his family and search for the treasure, but who is not tempted by money? Jacob was severely injured by Diego while trying to protect me. He wrote a letter for your father and gave me his journal and belongings. He told me to give all this to his son, but I guess your father never cared to open the box. He told me to run away and not look at him when he was dying. I was really scared. I managed to escape from the desert, where there was no food or water. I was injured too, but I managed on my own. I went back to the city and was in hospital for a while. Diego's men were looking for me, but luckily, they did not find me. I was discharged from the hospital and immediately decided to leave the place. I had lost any interest I had in this treasure and just wanted to get back home. I went back to Rottenburg and packed all my belongings. I decided it was wise not to live there as Diego's men were looking for me. I bought a house in Toronto and moved here. I was living a normal life until a few people approached me and decided to interview me about this treasure. It is probably the article you were reading. Trust me son, the treasure ruined my life," she said.

The three of us were devastated on hearing this. James, especially, felt bad for her.

"Why are you in a wheelchair? Is it because of the desert incident?" I asked.

She smiled. "No son, I have had severe back issues for years.

We realized that Julia didn't know our names, so we formally introduced ourselves. She offered us some tea, which we accepted.

She went into the kitchen. "Well, she's not that bad. She's actually very sweet and kind," James said.

'Yeah, but let's get straight to the point and ask her for the key to open the box," I replied.

Aaliyah and James agreed. Julia came back with the tea, and we drank it. To my surprise, it was really good. She kept smiling at us and we kept smiling back at her. There was an awkward silence between us for a while. I broke the ice.

"Look, ma'am, we read in the letter that we need a key to open a box, which supposedly contains the treasure map. We believe that you have it."

"Well, even after I told you my story, you still want to go after this treasure. I do have the key, but can I have a look at this box?" Julia asked.

We handed her the box from my bag, and she stared at it for a really long time. It was a rectangular-shaped box with an ancient engraving, I think, along with a few weird drawings and a mythical creature.

"Your grandfather and I had found this box in the church we visited in Brest. We decided to keep the map in the box and lock it, so it does not get in the wrong hands," she said.

We asked her if she recognized the writing and drawings on the box.

"Well, I have no clue, but I may know someone who can translate this," she said.

We were happy on hearing this and I asked, "So can you give us the key now?"

She told us to stop talking and follow her. We were kind of

confused but went along. She went towards the study room with wall-to-wall bookshelves. She pressed a button on her table that required her fingerprint and holy crap! The bookshelves moved apart, and a secret entrance appeared. It opened into a room that was entirely filled with portraits and paintings of sailors and pirates. There were a lot of books on the lost Drakon mines and multiple maps.

"Miss Julia, this is quite the treasure room!" James yelled excitedly.

She smiled. "Yes, I dedicated almost my whole life finding this treasure, but I gave up eventually."

"Wait so you did not give up after my grandfather died?" I asked.

"I did eventually, but I researched about its origin and found many myths. I visited multiple places and asked a lot of people, but I had no luck. I returned the books and valuables I found in Rio and Brest." Julia said.

"So, wait, if we want to find this treasure, do we have to visit all these places again?" Aaliyah asked.

"Unfortunately, yes," she replied.

Julia handed us the key and told us to open the box. Inside, there was a huge map that looked very old and fragile. Julia told us to handle it with care. The map showed four locations. The four main locations were marked with an X and there were a bunch of small dots and crosses surrounding those locations. The names of the four places were written in the same ancient text as the exterior of the box.

"If you are actually going to search for this treasure, I must warn you that you may face a number of enemies. But I believe you three are very strong," Julia said.

"Did Diego's men ever come back for you or the treasure?" Aaliyah asked.

"When I finally gave up on the treasure and went to Brest and Rio to return the valuables to their original resting places. I was hunted by Diego's men, but I managed to escape. I heard they went back to the desert and were never found again," she replied.

"Damn, you have really been through a lot," James said.

"Why was Diego shining blue and how the heck could he release blue beams from his body?" I asked.

"That is something that remains a mystery. I feel the caves in that desert have radiant energy in them. Whoever reads the text on the rock's channels that energy. Your grandfather died because of that," Julia said.

"Well, that's weird," I said.

"Wait, aren't you kids supposed to be in college?" Julia asked.

"Our university has given us two months' leave for projects," I lied.

"Well, I wish you luck in finding this treasure, but be safe. I have a meeting in some time, so I better get going," Julia said.

Our flight back to Vancouver was at 7 pm, but it was still only 4, so we decided to explore the city. I had never been to Toronto, but James had stayed here for two years so he took us to a decent restaurant. We had some good food and went to the airport. We told our parents that we would be back by 2 am, and that our project was looking good.

On the flight, we talked about our journey so far. "Wait remember the creepy guy who approached us in college and told us about the treasure?" James said.

"How could I forget? Everything started because of him, and I think we should call him back. We can't find this treasure alone, and that guy looked like he could help," I said.

Aaliyah and James agreed with me. We spoke for a while and the two of them looked calm, but I kept thinking about that weird figure who appeared in my dream. We landed at midnight and took a taxi from the airport. Aaliyah went back to her house, and James and I came back to mine. Luckily my parents were awake, so they opened the door and gave us something to eat. We were really tired and went to sleep immediately. We woke up extremely late the next morning, and were greeted by Aaliyah, who was waiting for us to wake up. My parents had already left for work. We got ready and quickly ate the sausages that my mom left for us.

"Now what do we do?" Aaliyah asked.

"Let's call that creepy guy." James said.

"His name is Julius, and I have his number in my backpack. I think he wrote it down on a piece of paper," I said.

James took my backpack and opened it. He read out the number and I entered it into my phone. Before I could dial, Aaliyah yelled, "Stop!"

“What, why?’ James asked.

“If we call this guy, he might tell us to meet him immediately. Before all that, I want to research this guy and find out what he does,” she replied.

We tried to Google him, but we only knew his first name. “Guys, he came to our university. He must have registered his name and information.” James said.

“Yeah, but that’s only with the security guard. Today is a holiday and he wouldn’t be there,” Aaliyah pointed out.

“He won’t be there, but the book will’ James smiled. He wanted to steal the book.

We argued for a while but realised we had no other option. We cycled to the college and luckily there were no cameras in the main gate. The security room was next to the main gate. We peeped through the window and saw the book.

“Let’s break the window and take the damn book,” James said.

“Are you mad? We will hurt ourselves and people will hear the noise,” Aaliyah said.

The gate was about 10 feet tall. He told us to give him a boost up and he jumped over the gate. He went to the other side, but the door was locked. “Yo, pass me a stone and I will break this lock,” he yelled.

We risked getting expelled, but I picked up a big stone and handed it to him through the bars of the gate. He looked like he did not care one bit and broke the lock. He entered and noticed the security cameras. We were all being recorded.

“Guys, I messed up. There was a camera in there, and I don’t know how to delete the footage,” James said.

I knew something like this would happen. I asked Aaliyah to give me a push and jumped over the gate. I was a computer science student, and it was easy to hack the system and delete the footage. I also disabled all the CCTV cameras in the college and took the register.

We finally found out the man’s identity. His name was Julius Calona, and he claimed that he was a businessman in Germany. He was fond of treasures and had pretended to be a visiting lecturer on the subject. We put back the register and jumped back up the gate. We could have gotten into serious trouble but now we knew who this guy was. We told Aaliyah about him and went back to my house.

We looked him up on Google and were quite disturbed. He had no social media and basically zero internet presence. But one article said he was a murderer and had committed serious felonies. We could not find more information, but he was sentenced to thirty years in prison and released within ten years for good behaviour.

We found a phone number online and decided to give it a call. He picked up and told us to meet him at Malrow's. We were a little scared and wondered if this guy was a good person or a bad person. When we reached, a waiter approached us. "Your table is right there, sir. Mr. Calona will meet you in a few minutes," he said.

We sat down, extremely nervous. I could only think about the article about this guy. Aaliyah and I did not order anything, but James asked for an iced cappuccino. Finally, Julius arrived. He sat down. "So have you guys decided?" he asked.

"Decided what?" Aaliyah asked him sarcastically.

Julius got really frustrated. "Listen kids, do you want to join this quest and help us find this treasure, or do you want to face serious consequences?" he said.

"Relax, we will join you on this so-called 'quest'. But who are you and who do you work for?" I said.

I got into big trouble with the cops when I was your age. I had given up everything and had no hope in life until Mr. Kaiser approached me. He was a rich businessman and was offering jobs to ex-cons like me. He explained that there was treasure gold in the lost Drakon mines, and that it belonged to his family. We had all heard stories about the mines, but we thought it was just a myth. He had been researching about for a very long time and it had made him crazy. We've been trying to find it for the last four years. He found out about your grandfather and told me to find you. He believes that you have information on the treasure," Julius said.

"Holy shit Julius! That is a lot to take in. So, this Kaiser guy has knowledge on the treasure?" I asked.

"Yes, but he does not tell anyone," Julius said.

"So, he wants our help in finding it?" James asked.

Julius nodded. "He has an offer for you, and wants you to meet him in Berlin," he said.

"We can't afford flight tickets to Berlin! Plus, we have family here, we can't just abandon them," I replied.

"You can take our private jet. Meet me tomorrow at the same cafe at 10," Julius said. He paid the bill and walked away.

"I don't mind going to Germany, but what if this Kaiser guy is dangerous," James said.

"Forget about -- how will my mom and Leo's parents agree to send us to Germany with a stranger we met a couple of days ago?" Aaliyah asked.

We decided to tell our families that we were going on a field trip to research our final projects. They didn't ask us any questions, and we didn't tell them when we would be back.

We woke up very early the next morning, even before my parents. We packed all our belongings and left the house through the window. After waiting for Aaliyah to sneak out of her house, the three of us walked to the café. It was a three-kilometre walk. We walked so slowly and talked so much that we reached the place at 8:00 a.m. we were two hours early, but the cafe was opened.

We were hungry so we ordered some breakfast and coffee. Julius arrived late, at 10.17 am.

"Sorry for the delay. I had some work to take care of. Your parents agreed to let you guys go to Berlin?" he asked.

"We didn't tell them anything." James said.

He smiled sarcastically. "Well, isn't that convenient. Let's get going," he said.

Julius's Mercedes was parked outside. We got in, feeling extremely nervous.

I wanted to know if my grandfather's craze for this treasure was actually real. I knew the desire for treasure was taking over me completely and I had no control over my actions. I was open to commit a crime in my college because I was so keen to find the treasure and left my parents without telling them because I was so keen on finding this treasure, I knew that I was becoming what I feared.

THE VILLAIN

Chapter 5

Kaiser's private airstrip was a two-hour drive away. Julius told us to rest for a while. James kept admiring the car, and Aaliyah fell asleep as she was really tired.

"Is this Kaiser guy a good person?" I asked Julius.

He smiled. "It's Mr. Kaiser to you -- and he is a wonderful gentleman and extremely trustworthy. He may get angry at times, but he wishes good for everyone," he replied.

I nodded my head, though I had a weird feeling. It was as if Julius was manipulated to talk about Kaiser like that. Julius put on some music and increased the volume to full. He had really good taste in music – the songs were by Metallica, AC/DC and John Lennon. James asked him, "Is this car yours?"

"No. The cars and the jet belong to Mr. Kaiser," he replied.

We finally reached the airstrip; sure enough, there was a private jet waiting for us. It was a luxurious experience. It was a twelve-hour flight, and Julius told us to rest and enjoy ourselves. The three of us spoke for a while, while Julius sat in the next seat.

When we finally reached Berlin, Julius told us that Mr. Kaiser would meet us the next day, as he had something important to take care of. He drove us to a hotel, where we got three separate rooms. He took off and told us that he would be back for dinner. The rooms were enormous and luxurious. I freshened up and headed off to Aaliyah's room. James was already there so we decided to call room service and order breakfast. The menu was in German, so we asked the man on the other end to help us out. He sent up a dish piled high with potatoes eggs, vegetables, and other delicious things. It was called hoppel poppel, a traditional German dish, which we learnt after devouring it. We had a lot of time to kill, and we could not leave the hotel. We watched TV for a while and relaxed. Julius finally arrived in the evening. He had brought dinner, and after eating, the two of us decided to share my room. I didn't mind, as the room had two beds anyway. I slept very late, but Julius slept pretty early. Even before he slept, he never spoke to me and was busy on his phone.

The next morning, Julius drove us to Mr Kaiser's house. Actually, it was not a house, but an estate, in the outskirts of the city. The entrance was guarded by a huge gate. When we approached, a man who was fully armed came forward and greeted Julius. He scanned his face in front of a screen and the gate opened. We could see the huge house at a distance.

When we finally reached the house, we were met by four security guards, and Julius whispered something to one of the guards. All of them moved away and Julius took us to the second floor. It was a huge mansion, decorated with fine things. The second floor had two rooms -- one belonged to Julius, and the other was Mr. Kaiser's.

"Listen, kids, before you enter the room: I want you to treat Mr. Kaiser with respect. Do not argue with him," Julius warned.

I found this weird but nodded my head. We went in, and I was suddenly stunned. The man sitting in the chair looked exactly like someone I had seen in a dream a few days ago. His left eye was covered with a black patch, and he had multiple scars on his hands. He was wearing a well-tailored black suit. His right eye was red, and just the sight of him scared the crap out of me. Julius walked out of the room and closed the door behind him. The three of us were shivering in fear as the man approached us.

"You kids must be Leo Schmidt, Aaliyah Thomas and James Anderson," Stephan said.

I was extremely nervous. "Uh, yes sir. Why did you get Julius to find us?" I asked.

"Leo, I know your grandfather had stumbled upon this treasure and that he, unfortunately died. I know you have his journal and the map. I need your help to find this treasure," he said.

"And what cut of the treasure do we get?" I asked.

"We split it equally, because without your grandfather's map, we can never find the treasure." he said.

I knew that Stephan was lying and wanted it all for himself. I wondered why he didn't just kill us, taking the map for himself. The fact that he decided to be generous and offered us a chance to find the treasure amused me. I had a bad feeling about him, but I was intrigued. We sat down in his chamber.

"I have done a fair deal of research, and even spoke to your grandfather's friend Julia." he said.

"How do you know about Julia?" I asked.

"Julius was keeping an eye on you guys and found out that you travelled to Toronto," Stephan replied.

"Wait, you met her after we met her," James said.

"I did not meet her, but Julius did. She refused to cooperate, so we had to deal with her," he said.

"What do you mean 'deal with her'?" James yelled.

Stephan laughed. "Well, we had to kill her. She had lived long enough anyways. If you do not cooperate, we will have to do the same to you kids," he said calmly.

The three of us were scared out of our wits and had no words. Aaliyah saw a gun and knife in Stephan's back pockets, but we could not escape now.

"So, tell me more about your grandfather's journal and show me the map," Stephan said.

We explained everything and took out the map. Stephan was completely amazed. I noticed that he could recognise some of the words on the map and was mouthing a few words. He did not speak a single word, though, and nodded occasionally when I was telling the story.

"So, the first three locations are Rio, Brest and Atacama, but the final one is yet to be found?" he asked.

I nodded. "We can head to the Atacama Desert from here and find the right cave," I said.

"We could do that -- but we will not. Let's visit Rio and Brest first. We need to destroy all the clues and make sure no one else finds the treasure," Stephan said. I didn't believe him: I felt that he just wanted the treasure all for himself.

What is your personal connection with the treasure?" I asked, curious to know.

Stephan got frustrated. "That is something I will not share yet. I do not trust you fully yet, but I will tell you everything in Brest if everything goes according to plan," he said.

I had a feeling that he was lying about his connection to the treasure just to get the map from me, but I had to stop making assumptions about him because he had not done anything suspicious until now. He grabbed the map and journal. He told us to follow him and went towards his bookshelf. I kept thinking about his connection with the gold, but how did he not know the locations on the map already?

He pushed a book on the shelf and the whole thing moved – the secret door opened into a room. We entered, but it was completely dark. He switched on the lights and holy crap! It was filled with artefacts, old maps, and knick-knacks that seemed connected to the treasure. He had portraits and frames of multiple sailors. I wondered why he did not contact me earlier about the map, and was about to ask him about it, when he suddenly started speaking.

"I was an honest businessman until a few years ago. I found out my family's history and learned the truth of how I was connected to this treasure. Now I am the only surviving member of my family, and I made finding it my sole purpose. I searched everywhere for the clues, but I could never find the final location. I got to know about your grandfather. I assumed you would have the map and his journal. Turns out I was right. Leo, I know I am troubling you, but I know you have a good heart and will help me – and I could use all the help I could get." Stephan said.

I felt bad for him, but still had a weird feeling in my gut.

"How did you get those scars, and what happened to your eye?" I asked.

"Two years ago, I was with my associates in Paris. They had told me about a lead on the treasure, but they were wrong. I was jumped by a couple of men with knives, who tried to rob me. I tried defending myself, but they ended up hurting me badly. I was sent to the hospital immediately, but my left eye suffered severe damage. I could not see from my left eye anymore and the scars on my hands were permanent. I wear a black patch to make it look cool, and sometimes my right eye turns red," Stephan said.

"I am sorry Stephan. It must have really hurt," I said.

"Anyway, we leave for Rio tomorrow morning. Go back to your hotel and get some rest. We will meet up in a safe location tomorrow morning," he replied.

We walked out of the room and told Julius to drive us to the hotel. Before this, I thought about forgetting the treasure and returning home, but Stephan changed my mind completely. We reached the hotel and the three of us went straight to Aaliyah's room, as Julius was sleeping in mine.

"Well, that was a lot to take in," James said.

"Stephan looked dangerous, but deep down he seemed vulnerable." Aaliyah said.

"I think it's all an act to win our sympathy. How can he just give us his family's wealth.?" I said.

"Yeah, you're right. Maybe he is just using us," James replied.

"I don't think so. He seems like a nice guy who just needs our help," Aaliyah said.

I felt like arguing, even though I really wanted to agree with Aaliyah and just think positively. We were tired so we went back to our rooms and slept. We had no idea how hard our life was going to get the next few days and the number of enemies we were going to make.

RIO

Chapter 6

When I woke up the next morning, Julius was already ready and waiting for us. As usual, Leo and Aaliyah took a long time to get ready. The four of us gathered in my room.

"So, what's the plan now?" I asked.

"We will be meeting Mr. Kaiser in the evening. You guys can have fun in the hotel until then," Julius said. He told us that he would pick us up in the evening and walked out of the room.

"What did he mean by 'fun'?" Aaliyah said.

"There is nothing fun in the hotel except food," I said.

We ordered a sumptuous breakfast and talked for a long time. But we grew bored after a while, so we just slept. Julius finally returned in the evening and told us to pack our bags, which we had already done.

We had no idea where Julius was taking us, but he had warned us that it would be a long journey. We had already been driving for an hour without stopping. Julius was silent, and I found that really fishy. After another forty minutes, we reached an old warehouse. It looked huge from the outside. Stephen Kaiser was waiting for us inside. He screamed with joy when he saw us. "Hello kids! I hope you're ready for the time of your lives!" We were confused and nervous but nodded and followed him to the back of the building.

Behind the warehouse was a huge area with a hangar. His private jet was inside.

"How many jets do you have?' James asked.

'Honestly, kid, I've lost count," Stephan replied.

We entered the private jet and were given some snacks. It was a fifteen-hour flight to Rio. Stephan sat next to me; I was forced to talk to him. He spoke to me like a friend and didn't ask about my family. The three of us rested, but Stephen was awake the entire time.

We finally landed in a private airfield belonging to Stephan's friend. We were greeted with cold drinks and taken to a nice guest house. His friend's name was Marcus, but he was not staying with us. The house had two floors; Stephan and Julius were staying on the first floor, while the three of us stayed on the second floor. It was 3 am in Rio, so we headed over to our respective rooms and slept.

I woke up the next morning and went down. Stephan and Julius were already awake.

"Why don't you wake up your friends and we can go out for breakfast?" Stephan said.

I nodded and went back up. We all got ready and left for breakfast with Stephan and Julius. We were sitting in a different car than yesterday's -- he and Julius had so many of them that I had lost count. We did not know where he was taking us, but it was most certainly a long drive from the guest house. We stopped at a roadside shanty for breakfast. It didn't look great from the outside, and we questioned Stephan's choice. But the pão de queijo that Stephan ordered for us was absolutely delicious.

"Well, since we are done with breakfast, let's get back to business?" Stephan said. We nodded.

"I read your grandpa's journal. He wrote about a library in Rio that had Mary Thompson's books on the treasure. We are going to find it." he said.

We followed Stephan back to the car and sat in silence. There were hundreds of libraries in Rio, and we had no clue which one my grandfather visited. We checked tens of libraries by noon, but didn't find any books related to the treasure. We even skipped lunch so we could keep searching. Finally, at what felt like the 73rd library, we found what we were looking for-Mary Thompson's book.

The librarian did not allow us to borrow it. When we asked why, she said that a woman named Julia Fraiser had given the book to the library a few years ago, and that no one could borrow it without her permission. She also said that we were the first ones to ask about it since it arrived there.

Stephan had already killed Julia, and I feared what he would do to the librarian. Luckily, he was silent. He called a number that the librarian gave us, and Julia's assistant picked up. I had no idea what they spoke about, but after, he handed the phone back to the librarian. She looked extremely scared. She just gave us the book and told us to leave immediately.

"Mr. Kaiser, what did you tell the assistant?" Aaliyah asked when we were outside.

Stephan laughed and ignored Aaliyah. I had a feeling that he threatened her on the phone.

Before going back to the guest house, we were starving and decided to stop for food. We stopped at a swanky restaurant where the staff already knew Stephan well, which was odd. Back in the room, I was really missing my parents and felt like going home, but I was stuck with a dangerous criminal and could not do anything. At night, Stephan and Julius left the guest house and told us that we could go out for dinner. He trusted us and assumed that we would not run away. We wanted the gold as much as he did, so we were definitely staying. Stephan gave us a generous allowance, so we searched for some fine restaurants in Rio. We found a good one nearby and walked there. We had our dinner and were casually talking until a notification pinged on James's phone. Stephan had taken all our phones in case our parents tried to track us down, but James managed to sneak in a second one. It was a message from an unknown number -- we would be killed within fifteen minutes. We were really scared and had no idea what to do. We ran back to the guest house. Stephan had not returned home yet and there were only three minutes left on the mysterious countdown. We all gathered in my room and locked the door. We heard the doorbell and loud knocking, but we did not go to open it.

"It's probably Mr. Kaiser at the door and this whole thing is probably just a prank, Leo," James said.

There was a loud noise that came from the first floor, and we got really scared. We heard gunshots and screams, and a man shouting, "Find those brats!" Someone started knocking on the room door and realised it was locked. "Boss, the kids are in this room. Let's break it," we heard a man say. We were really scared. My room had a window, so we decided to jump out before we were caught. We landed on the ground and were in pain. Aaliyah's ankle was twisted, and James's hand was probably broken. My head was bleeding, but we had no choice but to run. We had no idea where we were going. Seven men jumped out of the window too -- they looked pretty bulky. They had a lot of guns.

We ran for a really long time and finally got rid of them. We ended up at a beach, and there was not a single other person there. We had no way of contacting Stephan and asking for help. We were all injured pretty badly and found a clinic nearby. I carried Aaliyah as she was unconscious, and James was unable to move his hand. Luckily, we found a doctor there who was willing to treat us.

I slept for a long time after that. I woke up and saw that I was lying down on a single bed in a room which was smelling bad. I could not see Aaliyah and James, and I went looking for them. I had a really bad headache. I stepped out into the hall, and it looked just like the one in the guest house we were staying in. Julius and Stephan were sitting on the sofa.

"Where were you guys' last night? We were attacked by a group of men, and they were trying to kill us. Where are Aaliyah and James!" I yelled.

"Listen kid, that wasn't yesterday. I found you guys in a small clinic and took you to a different guest house. Your friends are still sleeping." Stephan said.

"What the hell are you into, Stephan? Were those men after you or me?" I asked.

"I am not the only one who knows about the map your grandfather found. There are many out there who want to hunt you down and get the map. My intel shows me that there is a gang here that's after you, but we haven't tracked down the leader yet. We can't leave Rio until we kill this guy," Stephan said.

"Well, let's not kill the guy, we could go to jail for that. I do not want to go to jail. Where are James and Aaliyah right now?" I asked.

"I will decide what to do with him. Your friends are on the second floor." Stephan said.

I ran upstairs and went to James's room first. He was still sleeping; being the idiot I am, I woke him up. He shouted in pain – he had fractured his hand. There was a cast around his left hand. I explained everything to him and went over to Aaliyah's room. She was already awake, but she was just starring at the ceiling. She had twisted her ankle. Fortunately, it looked better now, and she was feeling better. The three of us went downstairs slowly. Stephan took us over to the dining table, where there was a delicious breakfast waiting.

"I know one of you had a phone with you. That is how those men tracked you down. Who is this fool?" he asked.

"I am sorry. I had no idea there were men trying to kill us. I threw the phone in the ocean that day, I don't have it anymore," James said.

"Good riddance. You cannot get in touch with anyone or use any sort of phone. It is very risky," Stephan said.

"When do we leave for Brest?" Aaliyah asked.

"First, I have to get rid of this gang that tried to kill you. We can leave at midnight, eh?" Stephan said.

We nodded. "What do we do now?" James asked.

"James, you have a fractured hand, and Aaliyah has twisted her ankle. Both of you are not in a condition to do anything except rest. Leo can join me today." Stephan said.

He told me that he would pick me up in two hours and instructed me to dress formally. Aaliyah and James went back to their rooms, and I went back to mine. I took a hot shower after two whole days and felt great. I saw that Stephan had left a suit out for me. I wore it and it fit like a dream – honestly, I felt like a man. I wanted my parents to see me in it, but Stephan would never allow that.

Later, I waited for Stephan outside the guest house. He arrived in a Ferrari and told me to get in.

"You own cars in Rio too?" I asked.

"No, Leo, this belongs to my friend. He is going to help us track the gang down. We are going to meet him now," Stephan said.

I smiled. He smiled back and blasted some loud music. Stephan drove really fast and really well. We arrived at his friend's house, and it looked abandoned. It looked dirty from the outside, but when we entered, we saw that it was spotless inside.

It was built to make it look like no one lived there. We were greeted by Stephan's friend, Jake, who was a hacker. Stephan assigned him the job and went over to another room for a business call. Jake took me to the main room, which looked like a spy headquarters. It had multiple computers, laptops and screens showing footage from CCTV cameras.

While he did his work, the two of us chatted. He told me that he keeps moving locations so that he wouldn't get caught. He was wanted by the police for years, but they didn't even know what he looked like.

"Could you tell me what these men looked like and what car they arrived in?" Jake asked.

"Well, all of them wore black jackets and had pistols and knives. There were seven or eight men, from what I remember. They arrived in two trucks," I said.

"Did any of them look like the leader, or were they all wearing the same kinds of clothes and carrying weapons? At what time did all this happen?" Jake asked.

"I heard them call one guy 'boss', but I could not see this man. It happened two days ago, at about 8.30 at night," I said.

Jake smiled at me and started using his laptop. He hacked all the CCTV cameras near the guesthouse and found the footage from two days ago. He saw the two trucks and zoomed in on their number plate. He could not see where they went, but he somehow managed to get their location using the licence number. At the moment, they were at a bar close from Jake's house. Stephan was still talking on the phone, so we had to wait for him.

"Kid, you look pretty young. Did you run away from home?" he asked.

I nodded. "I live in Vancouver," I said.

"Well, I guess Stephan forced you to join him. Do you want to see if the police are trying to find you in Vancouver?" he said.

I nodded my head, and Jake began typing on his keyboard. It turned out the police had been trying to find us ever since we left. There were even photos of my parents and my friends on the internet. Everyone assumed we were dead, and the police closed the case just a few days ago.

"That is really messed up. You and your friends have your parents worried sick. Why is Stephan doing this to you? I thought he was a nice guy," Jake said.

Stephan appeared out of nowhere. "Leo, explain to Jake how you came here willingly and that I never talked you into it," he said calmly. He was right -- I had no choice but to nod.

"Jake, show me what guns you have, and we will head out to the bar," he continued.

Stephan had clearly been eavesdropping on our conversation for some time. Jake took us to another room which was filled with guns and knives. Stephan took two pistols and a few grenades. He also took a knife. Then, he handed me a pistol and a sharp dagger.

"Stephan, I really do not know how to use a gun. I am really scared to do this," I said.

"Do you want to kill them, or do you want to get killed? You must learn this the hard way, kid," he said.

I was scared out of my wits and wanted my mother there more than anything, but I followed Stephan to the car. We finally arrived at the bar, and we hid our weapons in our blazer pockets. We entered the bar, but it was full of people. We noticed a truck from the night of the attack parked outside, but the other two weren't there. We enquired about the owner of the truck from the bar manager. He told us that the owner was sitting in the VIP lounge and told us to go upstairs.

Before going, Stephan stopped me. "I will enter the lounge first and talk to them. But if they don't cooperate, I will give you a signal, and you come in and take your shot." he said.

Stephan entered the lounge. I had no idea what they were saying, but they were speaking quite loudly. Suddenly, I heard gunshots from the lounge and people started running out of the bar. I assumed that was my signal and ran into the VIP room. I saw three men on the floor, dead. Stephan screamed, "Shoot these guys, Leo!" I froze. He pulled me towards him and told me to duck. We were covered by the sofa and there were about eight men armed with guns and knives on the other side.

"I won't be able to handle all these guys alone. I need your help," Stephan said.

I was too afraid of the gun, so I took out my knife and threw it at one of the guys. Luckily, it hit one of them, and his eye started bleeding.

"Great, now you've wasted the knife. Use your gun!" Stephan shouted.

He had already shot down most of the attackers; there was only one left. I took out my gun -- it was already loaded. I took my first shot, and it hit one of them in the head. He died right there, on the spot. Stephan yelled, "Whoa, that is one hell of a first shot, kid!" I had no idea what I had done but all the men were dead -- one of them died because of me. I followed Stephan out of the bar, and we drove off in the Ferrari.

Suddenly, Stephan yelled, "It's not over yet, Leo. We're being chased!" Sure enough, we were surrounded by cars in all directions and were being shot at. Stephan was driving fast and ordered me to lower the window and shoot. I was dodging their bullets by luck and shooting at them, but I did not even manage to hit one target. "Hang on there, kid, I will take care of these men," Stephan said.

He took out a grenade from the dashboard and threw it at the cars. There was a huge explosion, and all the cars blew up as we drove away. To avoid the police, we saw on the way, Stephan gave me a mask and told me to wear it. He was a good driver, and we managed to stay hidden by driving through a narrow tunnel. Stephan took me through an unusual route, but we arrived back at the guesthouse.

"I was wrong about those guys. That is no ordinary gang -- we messed with the biggest crime lord in all of Rio. That was only half his army, and we still haven't got the leader," he said.

I was extremely scared and traumatised by what I had done. We entered the guesthouse. Julius, Aaliyah and James were together in the hall. Stephan informed us all that we were leaving for Brest in two hours and told Julius to arrange the private jet. Aaliyah and James tried talking to me, but I was lost in my own thoughts and felt like a criminal. I never thought in my life that I would have to kill a man. We packed our bags and left for the airfield. It was after midnight, and there was no one else on the road. Stephan and I went in the Ferrari, while Julius drove the others in a Maserati. We had almost arrived at the hangar when a truck suddenly appeared and rammed into our Ferrari. The car flew out of control and landed by the side of the road. Stephan and I were pretty banged up but managed to get out of the Ferrari.

A man got down from the truck. He looked big, and had multiple rings, chains, and a huge katana. Julius stopped his car and came up to us. Stephan yelled, "You stupid idiot! Go to the jet, Leo and I will meet you there. I do not want the two kids to see this bloodshed."

Julius drove away. The big guy kept walking towards us. I knew Stephan was about to do something terrible and just stood there.

Stephan ran towards the man and took out his knife. Stephan's knife was also big, but not as strong as the katana. They fought intensely. The man injured Stephan badly and was almost about to cut his head off, when Stephan grabbed the katana from his hand and chopped the other man's head off instead. It was 3:01 a.m. and not a single person was on the road. I just witnessed a guy's head getting chopped off in front of my own eyes.

"Let's get to the jet, Leo," Stephan instructed.

I did not say anything, though I suffered a few cuts and bruises too. We climbed into the truck, as Stephan's Ferrari was in a terrible condition. My friends were waiting for me at the hangar. Julius immediately ran to Stephan, and my friends came to hug me. We went inside – Stephan and I were bleeding. The others were talking to me, but I could not understand anything. All I could picture was the man's head separated from his body, which Stephan was responsible for. Even though the guy tried to kill us, guilt was eating me alive, and it hurt more than the injuries on my body. I did not understand why Stephan wanted me to see this bloodshed, but not my friends. It was as if he wanted to make me an animal. I was slowly turning into something that I had not even imagined, and I hated myself. Julius gave me some medicine and I slept for the rest of the flight.

BREST
Chapter 7

I woke up the next morning in the jet. We still had three hours until landing, and everyone was already awake, including Stephan. My leg had a deep cut which Julius had stitched it up. My head was aching, but I could remember everything that happened the previous night. Stephan was casually talking to my friends and acted as if nothing had happened. I still could not take out that horrible image out of my mind. Everyone were speaking to me, but I didn't reply. I was extremely frightened of Stephan.

"You are a bloody murderer! You plan on killing my friends, don't you?" I yelled suddenly.

Stephan exclaimed awkwardly, "Uh, Leo, let's speak privately."

I nodded, and everyone else moved towards the back of the plane, as I could not move my leg.

"I know that what happened last night is a lot to take in -- but we have more important work to take care of. I am really sorry to involve you in this mess," he said.

I started crying. "Who was that guy you killed?"

"His name was Brian Andrews. He was the biggest crime lord in Rio. He wanted the treasure too and was trying to hunt down his competitors. He had his eye on you from the start. When he received intel that you were in Rio with me, he tried to kill you. I was left with no choice but to kill him," Stephan said.

"Why did you make me kill that guy? You have no idea how I am feeling right now. I just want to hug my parents," I said.

Stephan looked annoyed. "Listen up, kid: I do not want you to turn out like me and kill people without any feelings. There are many out there who want to kill you, and all I want to do is to protect you so that we can find the treasure," he said.

"Wait, there are more guys like Brian who are trying to kill me?" I asked.

"Yes, and they will go to any lengths to get this treasure. Trust me, if they capture you and you do not give the information they want, they will kill you or torture you brutally. I am left with no choice but to kill all those who come in our way," he said.

"Why are you so cold blooded? Why do you care about me so much and why won't you tell me about the origin of the treasure?" I asked.

"I will tell you about the treasure once we finish talking to Mary Thompson's descendants and destroying the church in Brest" he said.

He smiled at me and went to the cockpit to talk to the pilot. My friends came over to me and Aaliyah asked, "Why were you and Stephan injured so badly? Who was that guy who rammed the Ferrari and why did you call Stephan a murderer?" I was surprised that Stephan hadn't told them anything while I was asleep, and I did not want to share the experience with anyone. I did not want them to get affected by it, so I lied. "I have no clue. I fainted after he rammed the car, and Stephan took care of the guy. I assumed he murdered him, but I was wrong. Stephan told me that he fought with the man and knocked him unconscious."

I didn't feel like talking anymore, and slept for some time as my head was feeling very heavy. I woke up just as we landed in Belarus. It was midnight in Brest. Stephan did not have any guest house here, but he booked us into a luxurious hotel. We were hungry so we ate there. The meal was nothing special, but it was filling. We headed over to our rooms, and I was restless the whole night as I had already slept for a long time. Everyone woke up early the next morning and we met in Stephan's room to discuss the plan.

Stephan told us that we would first meet Mary Thompson's great-granddaughter, who lived in Mary's old house. We would then go over to the church and destroy the secret room there to remove all trace of the treasure. Hopefully, no gang would come in our way, and we would wrap up quickly in Brest before heading over to the Atacama Desert.

Stephan had already tracked down the great-granddaughter and found her address. It would probably have creeped her out if we approached her out of nowhere, but that's exactly what we did, like a bunch of fools. We reached the place and rang the doorbell. A young and pretty woman answered the door.

"Who are you," she asked.

Stephan stepped forward, pushing us aside. "We believe you have something we are looking for. Can we sit and talk this out? This is going to take a while," he said.

She nodded and took us to the living room. There was nobody else in the house except her, which I found weird. The woman looked like a teenager, and the fact that she lived alone felt a bit suspicious. We sat down on the couch. "Why do you want to talk to me?" she asked.

"Your great-grandmother was Mary Thompson, correct? We are searching for information about a church she used to visit," I said.

"You are right, but I have no idea where the church is. I never spoke to the woman, my whole family hated her because she abandoned them years ago," she said.

"May we have a look at her room? We are sorry to intrude, but it is crucial we find the church. It's a matter of life and death," Stephan said. She pointed us to the end of a corridor. The others went inside, while the girl and I were alone in the living room. She told me her name was Marie, and that she was named after her mother.

I could hear the others talking in the room, but I did not want to leave Marie alone. I didn't trust her.

"Holy mother of God! I found it! I found the church!" Stephan yelled from inside. I ran in and saw Stephan holding up an old diary. The pages were half-torn, and it was dusty.

"What is it?" I asked.

"The church's location! All of Mary Thompson's findings are in this diary, but that girl sitting in the living room tried to hide it from us," Stephan said. "Go catch that girl!" Julius yelled.

I turned back to go back to the living room and found a gun pointed at my head. "Give me back the diary or I will blow your dear friend's brains out," Marie said. The gun was definitely loaded.

I was scared out of my wits and was almost in tears. Stephan was trying to decide whether to give her the diary or kill her. "Give her back the diary, Stephan! We can always get it back from her," James said.

Stephan slowly handed the diary to Marie, but she did not move the gun from my head. "All of you get out of my house, and I will let this damn kid go after you guys leave," she said.

Once they left, Marie let go of me and smiled. "You really thought I would tell you about my great-grandmother so easily. You are not the only one who is looking for this treasure" she said.

She looked very distracted and kept talking nonsense. The gun was still in her hand, but I noticed a knife on the sofa. She suddenly heard a sound from outside and looked towards the window. I quickly grabbed the knife and cut her leg. She started bleeding and fell down. She dropped the gun, and I grabbed it. I aimed it at her face as Stephan jumped in through the window. My friends and Julius also entered the scene. "Jeez kid, you are a natural! Do not shoot the girl -- hand the gun over to me," Stephan said.

I gave it to him, and he put it in his back pocket. "Now tell us why you tried to kill us, and why you didn't tell us about the church," Stephan asked Marie.

"I have been looking for this treasure since a few years. My whole family thought I was cursed by my great-grandmother because of it. I made a few powerful friends along the way and if you kill me, they will hunt you down. I knew you were close to finding the treasure, so I attacked you," she said.

"Well, that is wonderful. Such a young girl trying to find the treasure all by herself," Stephan said.

"I'm almost 30, you dimwit. I'll kill you and your friends!" Marie yelled.

"Good luck with that lady," James said.

Stephan told us to leave the house. I knew exactly what he was going to do. We heard a gunshot from inside the house and I was not at all surprised. "Did he kill the girl?" Aaliyah and James asked simultaneously. I did not want to answer the question and turned towards Julius. Stephan came outside and told us that he took care of her. "Let's get going to that church," Stephan said cheerfully.

Most of Mary's diary was about her journey in the Atacama Desert which was useless to us. The only useful thing in it was the location of the church. We followed the coordinates to the outskirts of the city, about 45 kilometres away.

I wondered how hard it must have been to find the church back in the 1800s without GPS.

It was a long and awkward drive "What did you do to the girl, Stephan?" Aaliyah asked.

He smiled nervously. "I knocked her out with a punch so she wouldn't come after us," he said.

"Why did we hear a gunshot then?" James asked.

"Can you guys stop interrogating me? We have to burn the secret room in the church and get the hell out of this god forsaken place before we are jumped by another set of men!" Stephan yelled.

There was an awkward silence for the next thirty minutes until we arrived at the church. It was surrounded by extremely tall walls. We saw the church at last through the gate. Luckily, the gate was climbable. We struggled a bit but managed to get to the other side. We walked up to the church -- it was locked from the outside. It looked decrepit, like no one had gone there for quite some time. Stephan pulled out Marie's gun from his pocket and shot the lock.

Inside, it looked like an ordinary old church. All the chairs had been demolished for some reason, and there were cobwebs and dust all over the place. "Search for the office room in which your grandfather found the key," Stephan said.

There were three rooms in the church, and two of them were locked. In the third room, there was a huge study table with multiple drawers. We opened all of them, and to our luck, we found a key that we believed would open the secret room. We walked up to the pulpit and found the secret keyhole. When we put the key in, it was the most wonderful thing I had ever seen. The space between all the chairs opened up and revealed a huge staircase leading down. "Your grandfather was a fool to leave the keys in the drawer," Stephan said.

I ignored him and walked down the stairs with everyone else. It was dark and Stephan sparked his lighter so that we could see ahead. It was a long staircase, and we kept walking for ages. We finally entered a room filled with portraits and paintings of sailors. Stephan seemed to recognise the sailors, but didn't say anything. We saw the map with the third location of Atacama marked on it. We also noticed a few guns – they must have belonged to Marie, as she had the co-ordinates of the church. I wondered how she could be so foolish to leave the key to the secret room openly in a drawer.

"Let's get upstairs and light this place up," Stephan said.

Upstairs, the key was still in the door. "Listen, Leo. As soon as I throw these grenades down there, turn the key and remove it from the keyhole," Stephan said.

He then threw five or six grenades down the gap, and I immediately turned the key and removed it from the keyhole. There was a huge explosion -- the floors of the church were able to withstand it, but the stairs leading down to the rooms were probably destroyed. "Well, let's get out of here and head to the Atacama Desert!" Stephan screamed with excitement.

We exited the church, and holy mother of God! A sniper bullet hit Julius's leg, and he fell down. We were being shot at from multiple angles. We noticed a small house inside the huge area and ran towards it.

"Who the hell are these guys, Stephan?" I yelled.

Stephan peeped and went into a state of shock. "I did not kill the girl – Marie. I shot her in her shoulder, but she must have managed to get back on her feet. She has come to kill us with her friends. We are in deep trouble, kids," Stephan said.

He passed me a gun and told me to shoot back. Aaliyah and James were with Julius. We were covering them from gunfire and shooting back at Marie and her gang. They had snipers and all we had were two pistols.

I looked around at the house. "Where are we?" I asked. "It must have been used by the priest, or Mary Thompson herself," Stephan said.

It was a small single-storey house. There was a huge cupboard in the room we were standing in. On instinct, I told James to open it and – luck was finally on our side! It was full of guns and knives, and even grenades. "Throw those grenades at those shits!" Stephan yelled.

I assumed he was out of grenades and threw two of them out the window. That held them off for a few minutes. Julius was bleeding, but we could not make a run for it until we got rid of our attackers. I gave Stephan an AK-47 that I found in the cupboard. What happened next was brutal and disturbing. He shot every single one of them and did not leave a single one alive, except Marie. She was already shot in the shoulder and could not escape. She surrendered and put her gun down. We surrounded her and Stephan grabbed her. "What is your problem, lady? Were you the one who shot my friend?" Stephan asked angrily.

"Yes, I did. I will make sure I kill every last one of your friends before finally killing you!" she said. Stephan raised his gun but put it back down and turned towards us. Suddenly, Marie got up and pulled out a knife she had hidden in her clothes. She ran towards Julius and slit his throat. Stephan yelled loudly and shot her in the head.

Aaliyah immediately fainted and James started crying. All this was starting to feel normal to me -- I believed that Stephan did the correct thing by killing Marie. I was turning into a stoic person, and that was not a good thing. Stephan ran towards Julius and started crying. There was a long silence. I felt bad for Julius, and was shocked that this would happen to him. I consoled James and woke up Aaliyah.

"Let's bury my dear friend and get out of this city," Stephan finally said. We did not want to argue with him. We drove to the nearest cemetery and found an empty plot, which we dug and lowered him into. Stephan told me that he met Julius a few years ago, but he was more than just an assistant. The two were like brothers.

Stephan drove us to the airfield where the jet was parked. As we were boarding, Stephan told us to wait. "Listen, kids, I am really sorry for all this. I understand if you want to get back home but remember this: you are wanted in three countries now, Canada, Brazil and Belarus. The government thinks we are an organisation, and the police are willing to shoot us down because of this mess. They have no proof of your involvement. If everything goes downhill, I will surrender and take the blame," Stephan said.

I felt bad hearing this, and knew he cared about us. He would probably not surrender to the police though; more likely, he would find a way to escape them.

"Will we ever see our parents again? Will we go to jail, Stephan?" Aaliyah asked.

"Yes, you can meet your parents after we find the treasure; and no, you will not go to jail. I will take care of the evidence and police, and you will go on with your lives as if nothing happened," he said.

We nodded and headed inside the jet. We sat down and my head felt heavy, so I decided to take a nap.

ATACAMA
Chapter 8

I woke up after a long nap and felt better. We were going to land in Calama in Chile in the next thirty minutes, and I was extremely tired. I had a lot of questions in my mind, but I was most curious about the treasure. And there was only one man who could give me the answers I wanted. I approached Stephan and sat next to him.

"You promised that you would tell me about the origins of the treasure. Can I hear it now?" I asked.

"Let's finish our business in The Atacama Desert and I will tell you about the treasure," Stephan replied.

I was not satisfied, but I was glad that he was at least planning on letting me in on the secret. We landed in Calama, where Stephan had arranged for a private car. He had booked five rooms in an expensive hotel before we even got there. Julius's death had deeply affected the four of us. I could see the pain in Stephan's eyes, but he tried his best to hide it.

At the hotel, we went to our respective rooms as Stephan told us to rest for a while. I did not speak with Aaliyah and James as they were extremely tired. I was not able to sleep and waited for Stephan to call me. He finally knocked at my door after a few hours and told me to meet me in his room. When I went over, Aaliyah and James were already there.

We sat down and Stephan started to speak. "I know what's happened in the past few days is a lot to take in, but in just one more week and we will be back in our homes." He told us that he would erase our police records and arrest warrants and told us the plan for the following day.

It was currently 10 am in Calama, and Stephan told us that a jeep would pick us up at noon. According to my grandfather's journal, there were multiple caves in the desert, and one of them hid the clue to the treasure. But we learnt some new information that scared us – there was a curse spelled out in ancient writings on the cave walls, and going to the correct cave would take us to the next clue, while entering the wrong cave would mean instant death.

It was a long drive into the desert, and even longer before we found the caves. Stephan told us that our driver could be trusted, but I was doubtful of that, as he kept looking at me and my friends. There were thirteen caves in the dessert, and all of them were located close to each other. We assumed that one of them was destroyed by my grandfather.

Stephan informed the driver and Aaliyah to stay inside the jeep. James, Stephan and I entered the first cave. There were insects everywhere, and they kept falling on our hair, we had no option but to move forward. Deep inside the cave, we saw a huge rock with ancient writing on it. Surprisingly, Stephan knew the language and when he read the words aloud, it sounded as if he was possessed. Nothing happened at first – but after a few seconds, we heard a rumble all around us.

"Run! It's the wrong one!" Stephan yelled.

The cave started to collapse pretty fast. We managed to get out, but we had to be careful the next time. We had to keep trying this dangerous method of trial-and-error for the next five caves. As we were driving around, I still doubted our driver but could not point my finger on what was suspicious about him.

The sixth cave reacted differently when Stephan read the text on the huge rock inside. It floated upwards and a deep voice said, "Jump inside." The rock broke into tiny pieces and we noticed an opening underneath. It looked like a deep tunnel.

"We found it!" Stephan yelled. "How will this tunnel give us the location?" I asked.

"I don't know. Let's jump in and find out," Stephan said excitedly. James was pretty scared and tried telling me not to go, but I wanted to know what was on the other side of this tunnel too.

Suddenly, we heard a gunshot -- the driver appeared inside the chamber, with a gun pointed at Aaliyah's head. "Oh, Stephan, you really believed that your brother would let go of this treasure. He's coming to kill you and take it for himself! Now, go down the tunnel and tell me the final location, or I will kill the girl," he said.

Stephen had a brother that he never told me about! But I could not focus on that. "How could you trust this guy?" I asked instead.

"I killed my brother -- that is why I did not tell you about him! I never knew this guy worked for him," Stephan said.

"Shut the hell up! The three of you go down the tunnel, now!" the driver yelled.

Having no choice, we slid down the opening. It led us into a room which had strange markings on every tile. On the other end of the room was a huge door. "Stephan, you are an idiot. What are we going to do now? By the time we get back up, your brother will be there with a gun against our heads," I yelled. "Yeah, you messed up big time," James added.

"Don't worry kids. I will kill my brother. I've done it once before, what's one more time?" he said, smirking.

"Okay, let's focus. Now, how do we get to the other end? These tiles have some weird markings -- if we step on the wrong ones, we might die," I said. Stephan continued to examine the markings and explained that each marking represented a different word. It looked like the same language as the writing on the rock in the cave, but I did not ask Stephan on how he knew it. "Follow me -- I know the correct tiles" he said.

We followed him as we skipped across random tiles, until the seventh one. Stephan stumbled and stepped on a wrong tile, and a sharp dagger came out of nowhere. It struck him in the shoulder. "Remove it from my shoulder, kid, fast!" he said.

He yelled in pain as I took the knife out. We still had to cross four more tiles. Stephan was luckier this time, and we reached the other side of the room. As we moved towards the big door, we heard a loud noise.

The walls slowly started closing in.

"There is no puzzle -- this was a trap! We have to break open this door," Stephan said. We tried to move it, but it was locked from the other side, and probably weighed a ton. The walls were moving closer to us, and we were about to be squished. Suddenly, Stephan punched the door with a lot of force, and it swung open. We ran inside but couldn't see anything as it was dark.

"How the heck did you do that," James asked Stephan. "Up to my forearms, my hands are made of titanium. They were reconstructed after an accident," he said. I knew he was lying about that. He changed the topic quickly. "We finally found it, kids! The map is right here!"

He swung his torch beam to the wall, which had a huge painting of a map. Stephan took down the frame and took the painting out. It looked old and delicate. At last, we had the final location: the Mokattam Cliffs in Cairo. This was fantastic news! But James and I noticed one strange thing about the map. It only showed two locations -- Atacama Desert as the first one and Cairo as the final destination -- instead of four. I thought it was weird, but I did not want to waste time questioning Stephan again. "Now we deal with my brother and head to Cairo," he said.

We saw a small opening in the room and went inside it. There was a huge ladder that led us into another cave. This one looked different from the others. Stephan pulled out his gun and handed me one, too. We put the map in his backpack and went out of the cave. We could see our jeep, along with Aaliyah and a group of men, in the distance.

Stephan fired a shot in the air. "Why would you do that," I yelled. "Let them come, I will kill every last one of them!" he yelled back. Meanwhile, the group of men sat in the jeep and came towards us. Aaliyah was with them. "Do not fire. I just want to talk," a mysterious voice said as the jeep approached.

A buff man with long hair and a well-trimmed beard approached us. He was wearing a suit -- in the desert -- and was not sweating even in the slightest. "So, we meet at last, brother. You have been of great help to me mate," the stranger said.

"Ryan. How are you alive? I killed you," Stephan said, confused.

"I was still breathing when you left me for dead that day. I was rescued by my men and taken to a Buddhist monastery. After a lot of healing, I began my hunt for the treasure anew. I found out recently that you found Jacob Weiser's grandson and the map. I do not want to harm you. Just give me the final location, and I will leave you alone," Ryan said.

"Let's get this over with, shall we," Stephan said, and threw a grenade at the jeep. It was blown to smithereens. Bullets started flying from all sides, and Aaliyah ran towards us. All of us took cover behind the cave. Stephan managed to kill Ryan's men and shot the driver in the head. Stephan's shoulder was bleeding – he was shot. Ryan did not have a gun and was just waiting while everyone else fought. "Well, you killed all my men! Now let's end this fight the old-fashioned way," Ryan said with a huge smile on his face. Stephan put down his gun and backpack. "Run from here and find Ryan's jeep," Stephan yelled.

James, Aaliyah and I ran away from the fight and searched for Ryan's jeep. Aaliyah knew where he had parked it and led us there. I could see Stephan and Ryan fighting intensely, but Stephan was not able to land a single punch. Ryan was quick with his movements. We finally found the jeep and I started it. We were quite far from Stephan, but the jeep got us there pretty fast. Stephan was getting pummelled. "Do not step out of the vehicle, kids," he shouted. I knew Stephan could knock this guy out with a single punch.

"You see, Stephan? While you wasted your time finding this treasure, I got stronger and made my men track you down," Ryan yelled. He was using a mixed form of martial arts and looked like he had trained for years.

Stephan grunted. "Fine -- you want me to kill you? I'll kill you!" he yelled and finally landed a punch on his brother. Ryan fell down and started coughing. Stephan punched him again in the face and, God, it looked like it was smashed to pieces. "Don't look! Start the jeep and be ready," Stephan yelled at us. I did not listen to him and kept looking at Ryan. Stephan kept punching his brother's head and did not stop. Stephan grabbed his gun and backpack. He got into the jeep and pushed me off the driver's seat. He started to drive and was almost in tears.

"Look, kids, I had no other choice. We have to leave Chile before the police start looking for us and more of his men come for us. Let's go to my secret warehouse in Italy and rest for some time," Stephan said.

We nodded, speechless. We finally made it out of the desert after a long drive and headed over to the hotel. Aaliyah nursed Stephan's injuries, but he was in pain for quite some time. We packed our bags and headed over to the airport. The private jet landed in Italy after a long journey. Stephan had his warehouse in Venice, which was a beautiful city. He had no friends in this country, so we booked a taxi and headed over to his warehouse. Inside, it was quite big and had six rooms. Stephan called the three of us to the hall and told us to sit down.

"Look, I know you have a lot of questions about the treasure and my brother. I promise to tell you all about it in the morning. Can we please sleep now as I am extremely tired," Stephan requested.

We were also pretty tired, so we headed over to our rooms. It was currently midnight, and I tucked in my bedsheets and slept. When I woke up the next day and went to the hall, Stephan was already sitting there. He looked better. He handed me a cup of coffee and told me to wait for my friends to wake up. The two of them came downstairs after a while. We sat down together and began one of the best and most interesting conversations I ever had in my life.

"Before you tell us about the treasure, Stephan, can you tell me why you and your brother tried to kill each other. Why did you hate each other so much and why are your arms made of titanium?" I asked.

"I can tell you about my brother, but not about my hands," he replied.

"That's fine." I said, even though I wanted to know. But I guess he wasn't comfortable sharing that story.

"My brother and I come from an extremely wealthy family. We were provided with everything by our parents except love. They were never around and were always busy with work. Sadly, they passed away when I was nineteen and Ryan was fourteen. Ryan continued his studies as he was still in school, but I dropped out of college and had to run my father's business. We had an uncle who guided us, but everyone called him crazy. He kept telling us about a treasure that was our supposed birthright to possess, but we never paid attention to him. He passed away when I was twenty-five. The company was doing well, and we were earning loads of money. Ryan soon dropped out of college and joined, too. The both of us headed it.

"We visited our uncle's house after he passed away. He lived alone. We went inside his room, and we noticed that he was obsessed with the lost Drakon mines. He had researched so much about it and wanted to find it, but he could never locate the map. All his research proved that our family was directly connected to the treasure. I never believed it and assumed my uncle was delusional, but Ryan became obsessed. He convinced me to meet the only living person who was close to my uncle, his ex-wife. We found out that she lived in Germany too, and we went to visit her. We asked her about the treasure and the information she gave us was mind-boggling. She told us that our ancestor was a pirate who had found this treasure along with his crew. It was said to be located in a mine, but no one knew where. I will tell you more about the treasure itself later," Stephan said and paused for a while.

He continued, "We thanked her for this information and returned home. We were in shock, but we believed her. Ryan and I continued to find more and tried our best to find the map, but we were out of luck. We then found out about Jacob Weiser, but he had been dead for years. We sent multiple letters to his son – Leo's father -- but we never got a reply. We even found out about Julia Frasier, but we could never find her address. We finally found the diary of my ancestor, who incidentally, was a pirate. We realised that the first location was Atacama Desert and decided to head there. I could see the greed in Ryan's eyes and his behaviour had been a bit off."

"Before we set off, we needed to learn to fight. We picked up a little mixed martial art and how to use a knife. We never used guns back then. After preparing for six months, we finally left for Chile. We booked an expensive hotel there and we decided to go to the desert the next day. Ryan finally showed his true colours that night when he suddenly attacked me with a knife while I was sleeping. I was lucky enough to dodge it. He kept hitting me, but I kept blocking. I never wanted to harm him, but he wanted to kill me. He suddenly stopped and told me that he had found a historian who would help him find the treasure. He told me that I was not needed in his quest and that he wanted to kill me. I was left with no option but to kill him instead.

It was the first time I had killed someone, and I booked a flight back to Germany immediately. Turns out, I was wrong, and I never killed him. He had his own set of muscle and friends back then. It was all in his plan to fake his death, and maybe he had found the final location to the treasure. When I thought I had killed him, I felt like I had committed a sin which I regret deeply and joined the army for ten years. I became inhuman, and I stopped thinking about it. I served my nation until it was time to look for the treasure again. I rebuilt my company and recruited many people, including Julius. Then we finally located you and had no choice but to bring your friends along. Well, that's what happened," he said, sighing.

I was trying to add up the math in my head. "You served in the army for ten years, so -- how long did it take for you to find the three of us," I asked.

"A month. I rebuilt my company six years ago and managed to make quite a few enemies and friends in that time," Stephan replied.

"So, you must be forty years old?" James asked.

"I am forty-two." Stephan said.

"Wait.... Aren't the first two locations of the treasure Rio and Brest? You just told me that it is Atacama now and I assume Cairo?" I questioned him with a lot of doubt.

Stephan told us to sit back tight and listen to it carefully. He finally told us about the treasure and holy shit! (read THE HUNT). Everything made sense now. A lot of questions were answered about the treasure.

We decided to head to Cairo, as we were well rested and felt better. Stephan warned us about the consequences of following him, but we ignored everything he said and were ready to end this. Stephan taught the three of us how to use a knife properly. He taught Aaliyah and James how to use a gun. I was already good at it. He handed them two pistols and a really sharp knife each. He gave me a shotgun and a pistol. He also gave me four sharp knives and a bulletproof vest. We left for Cairo by ferry.

It was a really long journey, and we finally reached the Egyptian city. We could not risk booking a taxi with all those guns in Stephan's bags. He was the one carrying the important stuff, like survival gear and a map. We only had our knives on us. Stephan had already rented a jeep in advance. It was close to 9 pm. We reached an expensive hotel, but it was nothing for Stephan.

I looked around the lobby. All the staff kept eyeing Stephan's backpack, and there was a man in the corner who was fair-skinned and tall. He had long hair and covered his face with a newspaper. His suit looked pretty expensive. It looked like he was staring at us, but I guess I was just hallucinating. The hotel manager was taking quite some time for the check-in and told us that it would take an hour as they were cleaning our room. We were quite hungry, so we went to the restaurant. Aaliyah and I tried hawawshi, which is basically pita bread stuffed with tender minced meat. James and Stephan had koshary, an amazing dish of rice, pasta and lentils cooked in tomatoes. We ended our flavourful dinner with a mind-blowing desert called konafa. It was much better than American desserts, I thought.

We went back to the reception. Stephan was handling the backpack with utmost care; he did not let it out of his sight. I noticed the same man reading the newspaper – he had not moved an inch. I knew something was odd about this guy. The hotel manager informed us that our rooms were ready and took us to there. We had the penthouse suite on the seventeenth floor. After freshening up, we met in Stephan's room.

"Okay, kids, listen up. The biggest mine in Cairo is in the Mokottam cliffs, which the map said. The mine is said to have coal and copper, but no traces of gold. There are multiple caves in the cliffs, but they've all been explored, except one. The only remaining hidden cave is deep inside the mine. The mine is very dangerous and is said to be haunted," Stephan said.

"Well, if that's where the treasure is located, we go to the mines and the cave," I said. Aaliyah and James nodded in agreement.

"Well, we will need TNT and a bunch of other explosives for this," Stephan said. He told us that he would arrange for them by the following morning, and we would be ready to go. I had noticed Stephan researching the mines late at night in his warehouse in Venice.

"Well, it's getting late now. Can we go sleep?" Aaliyah asked. Before Stephan could answer, the doorbell rang. We carefully approached the door and asked who it was.

"Room service," a man's voice said.

We had not ordered anything and were sure this was a trap. Stephan pulled out his gun and loaded it. "Who are you really, mate?" I asked.

"Open the door or I will have to break it, mate," he replied.

His voice sounded very familiar. Stephan opened the door, and holy shit, it was Ryan! He looked as good as new. I had seen with my own eyes when Stephan smashed his face into pieces, but this guy somehow survived it. Stephan and my friends were also in a state of shock. Ryan was the man reading the newspaper in the lobby! He took off his sunglasses, walked into the room, and sat on the sofa.

"Well, we are all in for a long chat, aren't we Stephan?" Ryan said.

But before we get into that, let me remind you of Stephan's crazy story, and how the treasure and his family were intertwined.

THE HUNT

Chapter 9

This epic tale dates back to the year 1613. There lived a great pirate by the name of Captain Fredrick Silverhand. He was coming of age and had completed scores of treasure hunts. He had a crew of thirteen men, who were fit and strong enough to fight anyone. Once, when they were between expeditions, they visited a pirate haven in France to rest for a while. Pirates did not have homes and kept shifting from place to place.

Silverhand had a very close friend in this haven, Charles de Dormans, whom he visited for a nice supper. His friend was an aristocrat, but the captain was a ruthless and rough man. He would interrupt everyone and eat without manners. They were talking casually until Charles said something that caught the captain's attention immediately. "Aye, captain, I am telling the truth! Let me get straight to the point. There is a great treasure, much bigger than any you have found so far. Its location is only known to the gods themselves! You must visit America, the New World, and retrieve a map that will take you to the treasure," he said with a huge smile.

The captain was delighted – he had wanted to do a final treasure hunt before finally sailing to the gates of heaven (or, more likely, hell).

"Aye, that is wonderful news, my dear Charles! I will pursue this hunt, but I cannot do it with a crew of only thirteen men. I would be grateful if you could lend me six more strong men," The captain said. "Aye aye, Captain," his friend replied.

Charles left immediately to assemble a team of six strong men. The captain left his seat happy, and went over to his crew, who were dining in a nearby lodge. He pulled them to a silent location and told them all about the treasure. He promised them that this would be their last adventure, after which he would be seeking pirate retirement, if there was such a thing. The crew was delighted. After a short wait, the group of six men arrived, along with Charles. "Ahoy, Captain. I have a ship waiting for you if you are ready to leave for this voyage. I will not be joining you, but my good wishes will be with you," Charles said.

"How dare you insult the love of my life! The Royal Bennet is in perfect condition and will not be replaced by that ship of yours," the captain growled.

Charles apologised and left. The captain met the six new men and introduced them to his crew. One of them met with the captain later and spoke to him with utmost respect, saying that he knew the ancient Kunza language of the Atacama people. The captain ignored him and gave instructions to set sail.

They took more than five months to reach the Atacama Desert. The gods tried to stop them with a series of obstacles and apocalyptic ocean waves, but nothing seemed to stop this crew. They were stronger than ever before and were ready to face anything for the treasure, but even they couldn't imagine what lay ahead of them.

They reached the spot where the ocean connects to the desert. They stepped onto land armed to the teeth with weapons, leaving three men to guard the ship. They were looking for a cave, as instructed by Charles. They walked for days, resting only for a few hours at a time. They started hallucinating in the heat, and even drank their own urine to survive because they ran out of food and water.

When they finally made it, they noticed a series of caves right next to each other. They went inside the first one -- it seemed quite ordinary, until they came upon a huge rock deep inside. A message written in an ancient text was carved on it, but no one knew to read it, except one. The Kunza man, named Santiago, asked the captain's permission to read it, and when he did, it sounded as if he were possessed by the desert gods themselves. He finished reading the message, and at first, nothing happened. Suddenly, the crew heard a loud noise, and the captain noticed the cave slowly started to collapse. "Run!" the captain shouted. They scrambled to get to safety, but one of Silverhand's original crew members did not make it out.

The captain was furious. "What cursed thing did you read," the captain yelled at Santiago.

"Captain, I read what the stone said exactly. Out of all these caves, there is only one that will show us the map. This ancient treasure is known to Chilean tribes for centuries, but no one dared go against the god who protects it," he said.

"What did the writing say, exactly? Tell me!" Silverhand said.

"'The one who stumbles upon the treasure and is not deemed to be worthy will be killed by the great gods themselves," Santiago replied.

The captain told Santiago to find the correct cave and sent three other men with him. After many failed attempts and the death of six men, they eventually managed to find the right cave.

They reached the mouth of last cave in an exhausted and traumatized state. But before they could enter, suddenly, they noticed six blue shining objects approaching them from a distance. The crew was scared out of their wits and gathered next to each other. As the figures approached, the captain noticed that they were none other than his men who died. Two were from his original crew, while four of them were recruited by Charles De Dormans. "What sorcery is this! How are those men alive," Silverhand exclaimed.

The shiny blue figures ran towards them. Silverhand and his remaining crew managed to escape, except for one, unfortunately. The otherworldly figures then suddenly exploded in a blast of light. The captain and those of his crew who were still alive were in a state of shock. Silverhand knew he was messing with a power equal to God, but he ignored it and entered the right cave. Inside, they found a huge rock like in the previous cave, only this one was broken into tiny pieces. There was a small opening underneath, which they all slid into. It was quite deep. At the bottom was a room with a huge door on the other end. The floor was covered in tiles that had ancient Chilean writing on them. Santiago knew the language fluently and managed to solve the puzzle and get the crew past. The door magically opened into a room. They noticed a huge map in the middle, with two locations marked on it – the desert in South America, and the cliffs in Egypt. Captain Silverhand was about to take the map down, but Santiago stopped him. He was worried that the map was booby-trapped, but it was not.

They spent three days in the desert, returning to their ship. On the way, they managed to find a small oasis and filled their wooden bottles with water. They returned to the ship and were greeted by the three men onboard. Silverhand and his crew were so hungry upon their return that they finished all the food on the ship. They restocked and rested up before beginning their voyage to Egypt.

When they reached Cairo after a long journey, they disguised themselves as commoners to blend in. The people there were as pure as daylight, but the captain and his crew were raucous. They kept disturbing the peace and questioning them about the Mokottam cliffs. After much difficulty, the pirates finally acquired the coordinates of the cliffs and began their journey there.

It was a steep and difficult climb, but it was nothing for the strong pirates; they were ready to do anything for this treasure. They finally made it to the top of the cliffs and laid eyes on the mines. There were multiple interconnected caves. A few locals said the mines only had coal and copper, but the pirates knew this was false. They noticed one cave that was not connected to any other, and they knew that this was the place they were looking for.

The entrance to this last cave was blocked by huge wooden structures. They could not move these and had to blow them up with grenades. They all took a step back as the grenades exploded. The entrance of the cave was now clear, and they finally entered.

It was a deep cave, and during the long walk, they kept getting lost. It was more like a maze than a cave. After multiple turns and dead ends, they finally made it to an open area. There was a huge opening in the floor, similar to the one in the desert.

They went down, down, until their heads were spinning. They knew they were way below ground level when they landed onto a platform, below which was boiling magma. A series of challenges stood between them and the door on the other side. If they messed up, they would fall straight into the magma.

Luckily, Santiago's knowledge of the Kunza language saved them. The first challenge was similar to the tiles in the cave. Once they all got past safely, another challenge awaited them. This time, the tiles each made a sound, and the trick was to only step on the tiles with the same corresponding tile. Santiago once again took the lead, somehow finding the correct ones and making it across. The second door swung open by itself and led onto a long bridge. In the distance, something was shining.

"Captain, we found it! There is gold over there! Shiver me timbers," one of the crewmen yelled.

The others started yelling loudly too; they were happy. They began to run across the bridge, but Santiago tried to stop them. He turned to Silverhand. "Captain, run! These dimwits stepped on a trap. This bridge is going to collapse!" Santiago yelled.

They ran for their lives to the far side of the bridge as it collapsed. Although the captain was old, he was able to match Santiago's speed and made it to safety. The bridge was collapsing quite fast, and only four men were able to make it alive. What started as a crew of nineteen men was down to four. The bridge crumbled into the liquid below, which looked like poison.

But they did not pay much attention to that. In front of them was the most beautiful sight they had ever seen. Piles and piles of gold! The captain hadn't laid eyes on so much gold ever before in his life; this was probably the most valuable treasure in history. The captain was about to touch one of the gold necklaces next to him, but Santiago stopped him. The others didn't listen and continued to touch the gold and wear the beautiful jewellery. Suddenly, they heard a mysterious voice. "Silly peasant! You are not worthy of this treasure. You shall burn for eternity," it said.

A bunch of skeletons suddenly turned up – they had climbed up from the poison! They attacked the sailors who had touched the gold and tore their skin apart. Only their bones were visible. The captain and

Santiago were scared out of their wits.

The mysterious voice now spoke to them. "Oh, worthy ones! You have completed the challenge I have laid upon you mortals. As a reward, you may take ten bars of gold, and nothing more. If you take more, you will suffer for all eternity!" it said.

The captain and Santiago were delighted. Though they wanted to take all of it, they stuffed ten bars into their pockets. When they finally exited the cave, they ended up at the top of the Mokottam cliffs. They had witnessed something miraculous that no one would believe. They took the gold and made it back into the city.

After that, Silverhand and Santiago became very close friends, and were done being pirates. They were both too old for more adventures, and wanted to retire, if that was a thing. They made it back to the pirate haven in France, where they met Silverhand's old friend, Charles de Dormans. They told him the whole story, which put him in shock. He bought the gold from them for a whopping twenty thousand euros, which would evaluate to 1.5 million euros today.

The two men were no longer pirates; they were just two old friends who wanted to do one last thing before returning to their families. They did not dare to go back and disturb the great god who guarded the treasure, but they did want their respective families to find it and experience the magic themselves. Both of them wrote details of their journey in their diaries, but never gave away the location. If their descendants were worthy, they would find the landmarks on their own, they figured.

Their story had become famous among other pirates, and many wanted to find the treasure for themselves. So, the two friends decided to create a false map pointing to places like South Africa and Greece as the two locations to the treasure.

However, as time went by, Santiago could not forget about the treasure. He became greedy, and did not want Silverhand's family to find it. He wanted it for his own. So, he stabbed his dear friend while he was sleeping. But Santiago did not know that Fredrick had already handed his diary, which did not include the final location, to his wife. Santiago left the fake map near Fredrick's body to throw the others off.

Santiago ended up moving to Brest with his family. He built a small church and lead a happy life. However, he never forgot the treasure. He eventually built a secret staircase that led to a room under the church. He hung portraits of his fallen crewmates and created a map highlighting Rio, Brest, and the Atacama Desert, leaving the final location a mystery. He left his diary there, so whoever would find the key to the secret room would also find the treasure. He even wrote a book about the mines, under the name of Santiago Thompson. He died a few years later, happy and old.

Fredrick's diary eventually made it to his great-grandson, Stephan. The story was passed down from generations, but no one believed it. Stephan's uncle was the only one who paid attention, but he never went looking for it.

Stephan never knew that Santiago had a living descendant -- Mary Thompson -- until he read about Jacob Weiser. Mary had somehow found the secret room in the church and read her ancestor's journals. No one in her family believed her, either. They thought her a lunatic and abandoned her. But she continued her quest, until her violent death in Atacama.

So many things added up now, but there were more questions still to be answered. We would soon be able to put the puzzle together.

THE MYSTERY UNFOLDS

Chapter 10

Now that we know about the treasure, let us get back to the present. Ryan was in front of me, though I had seen him die in front of my own eyes. His head was literally smashed into pieces and there was blood all over his body. There is no way anyone could survive such a brutal injury. He was sitting on the sofa, wearing a fine black suit that looked pretty expensive, and those sunglasses were a work of art. He had a Patek Philippe Nautilus watch. His face looked clear and had sustained no damage, surprisingly. He took off his glasses and looked at the four of us.

"How do you keep surviving, little brother?" Stephan asked, amused.

"I will tell you, but you may not believe it," Ryan said.

"Stop wasting our time and get on with it," Stephan said in anger.

"Okay, you asked. When Stephan and I were training for Atacama, I got a call from a mysterious historian three weeks before heading to the desert. She said she wanted the treasure as much as us. I couldn't figure out how she knew about us. She told me that we would need to learn an ancient Chilean language, and that she would teach me. But she would do so only on the condition that I kill Stephan and split the treasure with her instead. I loved you, Stephan. But I love money more." Ryan said.

"I agreed to her proposition and waited for the right time. We headed over to Chile and I tried to kill Stephan while he was asleep one night, but I was the one who was stabbed in the chest. You thought I was dead, Stephan, but I was not. The historian found me and took me to a monastery to recover. When I woke up three weeks later, she was beside me. I noticed my wound had healed and I felt stronger than ever before. Julia scolded me for not killing my brother but said that her men would take care of that," Ryan said.

"You idiot! The only reason I survived was because I joined the army. If I hadn't, I would be dead," Stephan said. He looked frustrated and angry.

"Don't interrupt me," Ryan said. He continued, "Julia told me that she found the treasure and even tried to touch the gold, but she was deemed unworthy. The gods killed her men but pitied her and instead cursed her with immortality. She was horrified and asked if it could ever be removed. It could only be done if she mixed her own blood with that of the descendant of one who had touched the treasure. "

"The historian never told me the location of the mines, but she told me that she searched for the descendants for a long time before finding me, Stephan, and Grace Thompson, Marie's mother. She watched us from a distance when we were children, waiting for us to come of age. She approached Grace when she was seventeen, but Grace was not at all interested in the treasure," he said.

"Wait, Ryan, how do you know about Marie?" Stephan asked.

"I have been tracking every single move of yours for the past three years. You didn't have to kill her like that," Ryan said. Before Stephan could respond, he continued with his story. "I asked Julia to teach me Kunza, but she was slowly going mad. She ended up slitting her throat with a knife – whether it was a blessing or a curse, I was there, and her blood fell on me. I didn't know it made me immortal! When I would cut myself, my wounds would heal magically within a minute," he said.

"Ryan, you're immortal?!" Stephan yelled.

"Stop interrupting me! Once I had this power, I built my own crime syndicate. I'm the one who sent all the assassins after you guys. I enjoyed this immortality; I realised its consequences. It makes you strong physically but destroys your emotions and feelings. I never felt any sorrow for the men and women I killed for no reason. The only woman who ever loved me left, because I could not show her any love. I was slowly becoming emotionless, but I could not do anything about it. I continue to research about a cure for this and I could not find anything. I decided to find the mines and treasure, as the problem started there and will probably end there, too. I've been tracking you for the past three years -- I never wanted to harm you in the desert, but you kept firing at me like a super cop," Ryan said, his voice getting louder with emotion.

"What guarantees that you won't transfer the curse to me," Stephan asked.

"If I wanted to do that, I would have done it long ago. I do not want anyone to suffer like how I suffered. This is the conclusion I have come to with the last of the emotions left in me. I didn't even want to transfer it to Marie -- I do not wish such a fate for even my worst enemy," Ryan said.

Stephan nodded. "Well, let's try to get some rest now, is that okay? We have a huge day ahead of us," he said. I was not okay with this and had a lot of questions. "Who were the tribal men who gave the map to my grandfather, and who wrote that book in Rio?" I asked.

"Well, that will remain a mystery for some time, young man. Let's sleep now," Stephan said.

"No, Stephan. I know the answers and I would like to share them with him," Ryan said.

"Well, out with it," I said.

"To answer that, we have to go back to Mary Thompson. As you probably know, she found the letter and secret room created by Santiago. She ended up going to the desert and even learned Kunza. She even knew which cave was the right one. But she wanted to make sure someone would find this treasure if she did not make it out alive. Her own family never wanted it. So before going to Cairo, she went to Rio and published Santiago's writings as her own, because she wanted fame. She even made a fake map that only had Rio marked on it. She ended up handing this to some tribesmen in the Amazon, who later met your grandfather, Jacob Weiser," Ryan explained.

I was taking all of it in; I had so many questions. "My grandfather's journal says that Mary died in the desert," I said, not knowing where to begin.

"Well, that's a bunch of bullshit. She went to the caves and even found the treasure, but she was stupid enough to touch it and was deemed unworthy. You don't even want to know what they did to her," Ryan said with a smile on his face.

"Wait, how do you know about Marie," Stephan asked again.

"I found out about her a few years ago and felt bad for her. She went crazy over the treasure, but her family never approved of it. They left her in Brest, in Mary Thompson's very house, assuming the house was cursed. I found the caves with her help, as Mary's diary stated everything perfectly, but not knowing Kunza slows us down. I left the girl and told her to guard the diary, but you ended up killing her," Ryan said.

"I had no other choice. She killed Julius, and even tried killing us," Stephan replied.

I could see he did not care for her as he just laughed about it.

"Hey, Stephan, don't you know Kunza? How did you learn it," I asked.

"After the army, I visited my uncle's house in Frankfurt again. I found a book there which taught me the language. It took more than three years, but I finally got the hang of it," he replied.

"Wait -- I had another question. We know how your ancestors found the treasure, but whose was it first? What kind of gods are you talking about," I asked, still confused.

"Ah, kid, that's a tough one. The short answer is that nobody knows," Stephan replied. I was still not satisfied, but it was getting quite late.

Aaliyah thought so too, and said, "Well, this has been fascinating, but can we please go sleep now? Its 2 am."

We only slept for a couple of hours. By 4 am, we were assembled in Stephan's room. I was drinking my regular black coffee.

"Don't worry about the explosives and guns. I have it arranged," Ryan said.

We checked out of the hotel and loaded the weapons in the Jeep. Ryan changed into a jumpsuit that hid many dangerous toys inside. We were finally ready to grab the treasure.

THE LOST DRAKON MINES
Chapter 11

No one said anything on the drive over, as we were all anxious. We finally reached the foot of the cliffs, from where we had to begin walking. We were all tired, but somehow walked for a whooping two hours. The path was full of snakes and insects, but they were not dangerous. We finally reached the top of the cliffs and looked around. The view of Cairo was breathtaking.

There was an ancient quarry on the other side, which was where the caves were located. We had to climb down the rocks to get there -- it was risky and dangerous, but we did it. We looked for the cave with the wooden structures outside it. We ended up finding it on the other end – the wooden structures were two enormous rectangular blocks. Both James and Stephan tried to move it, but they were unlucky.

Ryan had a huge stick of TNT with him. He put it near the blocks and told us to move away. There was a huge explosion, and a cloud of smoke rose over the place. We had to wait for the smoke to clear before we noticed that only a little part of the blocks were broken, but it was enough to enter the cave.

"That is definitely not wood!" Stephan said.

Ryan laughed before turning serious. "There is something important I must tell you before we enter," Ryan said.

"Yes?" all of us said in union.

"These are called the Lost Drakon Mines because drakon is the Greek word for dragon. No points for guessing what might be waiting for us inside," he said.

"Stop scaring the kids and get inside, Ryan," Stephan yelled.

We entered the mouth of the cave; it was completely dark. Ryan put his lighter to a torch on the wall and it lit up, and we saw the weirdest thing. The wooden blocks magically reassembled themselves and blocked the cave again. We had no way of escaping, and knew this was the right place.

We walked for a long time and came upon a lot of dead ends, until we reached an open space. There was huge rock with some writing on it. We went near it – the writing was in Kunza. "Only the worthy shall find it. Others will suffer and die," Stephan read.

Suddenly, the rock broke into pieces and revealed an opening leading down, just like in the cave in the Atacama Desert. We went down and reached a room with a beautifully carved gateway on the other side. We had reached the room with the tiles.

Before stepping on one of them, Ryan threw a stone at a wrong tile. A spear flew through the air from the walls.

Luckily, with Stephan's knowledge of the language and Ryan's knowledge of the diaries, we knew which tiles to step on and made it to the other end safely. The door didn't budge, but Stephan said the Kunza word for 'open', and it swung open. We were so close to the treasure.

On the other side of the door was a long stone bridge, designed in the Gothic fashion. It reminded me of a dungeon. Below it was a river, but instead of water, it was flowing with a weird yellow liquid. It was boiling.

"What are we waiting for? Let's cross," Ryan said enthusiastically.

"Wait, you idiot. Don't you remember, the bridge has some puzzle we need to solve," Stephan said.

Ryan ignored Stephan and ran. "Follow him, quick, the bridge is going to collapse," Stephan yelled. We ran as quickly as possible -- the bridge had already started to fall apart. Stephan was cursing loudly at Ryan as we raced to the other side. The bridge gave way just as we reached safety, but Aaliyah was yet to catch up to us. She was so close – I told her to jump, and she did. I grabbed her hand and brought her up.

We brushed ourselves off and turned around – the most amazing sight awaited us.

All we could see was gold and lots of it. There were gold coins, gold statues, gold chains, gold bars and so much more. All of us were so happy and could not wait to get our hands on the gold.

We were mesmerized, but Ryan reminded us not to touch any of it. Suddenly, we heard a mysterious voice. "O worthy ones! You have completed the divine conquest laid upon for mortals. Each of you can take only ten bars of gold and nothing more. If you show greed and take more, you will suffer for all eternity," it said.

Since there were five of us, we could take fifty gold bars! I began to think of all the things I could do with the money as we stuffed our backpacks. Once they were full, we held the remaining bars in our hands.

"O powerful ones! I am cursed with eternal life. I have suffered for too long. How may I remove this?" Ryan asked.

"How dare you question our authority! Immortality was a blessing bestowed upon you, and you call it a curse. You are arrogant; the one way to remove it is to fight the immortal skeletons," the mysterious voice said.

Great, now we had to deal with immortal skeletons too! We told Ryan to forget about it and leave. Ryan ignored us and went towards a pool of the same boiling liquid as the river. Ryan told us all to dip our swords in the liquid. It made the blade feel stronger.

"Fight the great immortal skeletons and remove your curse," the voice said.

"What did you do Ryan," Stephan yelled.

"Help me remove this curse and I will never disturb you again, mate," Ryan replied.

Just then, we saw something white rise up from the river below. The skeletons! We knew we had messed up, but we had no choice but to fight back now, or we would be dead. There were about twenty of them, which made the fight difficult. We managed to slay all of them, thanks to our newly strengthened swords.

We were finally free from the skeletons! We were exhausted but happy, until Ryan said, "I still feel the curse is upon me."

"Guys, what is that coming towards us?" Aaliyah asked.

We looked towards the bridge and were startled. There was an army of a hundred skeletons approaching us -- and in the distance, a literal dragon. We had no idea how a dragon managed to come in, until I remembered Ryan's warning about the mines.

"Let's run away," Stephan said. He was scared.

"There is no light coming in from the outside, which means there is no escape until we beat these creatures," Ryan said.

"I will go find an escape route -- you guys fight these creatures," Aaliyah said and left us.

We were four people up against an army of skeletons and a freaking dragon. We were a little scared, but we were ready to take down these creatures!

THE FINAL BATTLE
Chapter 12

Ryan told us to give our all and reminded us about the magical swords. But James was extremely frightened and did not move an inch. The sword dropped from his hand, and he started shaking. Stephan pulled him to the side. It was just me and Ryan taking down the creatures. The skeletons kept running towards us and were close, but the dragon suddenly stopped.

We slowly started taking down the skeletons. They did not manage to touch us, and the weird thing was that they came at us one at a time, which made things easier. The skeletons were all different from each other. Some were tall, some were short, and some were even missing a few bones. A few even spoke, which scared us, but we immediately took them down. The dragon was sitting on the bridge and had closed its eyes. I knew something bad was about to happen.

Ryan noticed that the skeletons were coming from a portal, and they were not going to stop. Stephan was trying to wake up James, who had fallen unconscious, and I had to go close to the portal. It was close to where the dragon was, but I decided to step up and made my way sneakily. Ryan was distracting the skeletons, and I managed to get to the portal from the other side. The skeletons kept coming but there was no way to close this portal.

"You'll have to enter the portal!" Ryan said.

"No way! These skeletons are rushing forward with swords, I'll be killed," I screamed.

"Just do it Leo," Ryan replied.

I had no choice but to listen to this fool. He threw me an umbrella to use as a 'shield'. I held it in front of me and went in. I had to make my way through the skeletons. They managed to bruise my left shoulder, which then started bleeding.

The portal led me into an open area which looked like a forest. The skeletons were rushing down a mountain towards the gateway. The whole area was filled with trees and beautiful flowers. The main thing I saw was a huge volcano that had just erupted, and the skeletons were coming from there. I still could not find a way to close the portal and went back to the dungeon.

"Any luck?" Ryan asked.

"No, I don't know what to do," I said.

Ryan told me to come over to his side and help fight the skeletons for the time being. I knew the dragon, which had closed its eyes now, was the key to closing the portal. James finally woke up and came back to his senses. He grabbed his sword and joined us, along with Stephan. We kept fighting the skeletons until Ryan suddenly stopped swinging his sword. He was bruised and hurt but kept healing magically.

"Ah, this is boring! Let's provoke that dragon," Ryan said with excitement and struck his sword on the dragon's face.

"Not the dragon, you idiot," Stephan yelled.

The portal closed on its own and all the skeletons vanished. My injury on my left shoulder healed itself. Suddenly, the dragon's eyes opened, and it spoke. "So, you must be the brave one cursed with immortality," it said.

"Yes, that's me. I defeated the skeletons; now how do I get rid of this curse?" Ryan asked, like an idiot.

"Well, it's quite simple, young man. You have to defeat me," the dragon said and grinned.

Stephan told James to run and find Aaliyah. He threw his sword to Ryan and ran away. Stephan and I were pissed off at Ryan, but we could understand his need to remove the curse.

Suddenly, the dragon gave Ryan's sword back to him and flew up, vanishing in the darkness.

"Where the hell did it go?" Ryan yelled.

"Look here," a voice said from the dark.

The dragon reappeared out of the blue and released a column of fire from its mouth. I used the umbrella to guard myself, and luckily, it was no ordinary one. Its special fabric withstood fire. Stephan covered his face with his metal hands, but he got hit by the fire in the stomach and legs. He was badly burned but did not complain once. Ryan's jumpsuit was apparently fire and bomb-proof too.

Ryan used his hand to wipe his forehead, and noticed his arm was bleeding. It didn't heal automatically. We were shocked upon seeing this.

"How am I bleeding? I never bleed for more than a minute," Ryan said.

"This is a battle to the death. Your powers are nothing to me, you shall fight me like a mortal," the dragon growled.

It flew back to the bridge and sat down. The dragon was cooling down after releasing all the fire. It looked like its throat was burning from all the fire it breathed. I knew at that exact moment that the dragon could be defeated.

"There is no way we can defeat this dragon!" Stephan yelled.

"Let me make the battle a little easier, since you insist," the dragon said.

Its form slowly started shrinking and transformed into that of a human. The dragon was literally a man now! He was in all black clothes and was even wearing black shades. His hands were glowing red and looked bloody.

"Let's finish this," the man said and sprinted towards Ryan. He punched him on his stomach, and Ryan fell over the edge. He managed to use the grappling hook and get to the other end of the bridge where the treasure was. We noticed the bridge was falling apart and hopped through the remains of the bridge and joined Ryan. The man had vanished -- we could not see him. We assumed he had fallen over the edge too, but he appeared out of nowhere and punched Stephan's face. His face began to bleed.

Ryan was still lying on the ground, in pain – he had puked out blood. I was the only one the dragon-man did not lay his hands on, and I knew exactly what to do. He sprinted towards me, and I yelled loudly.

"Stop! Let's be reasonable. I have a question to ask you," I yelled.

"What is it, boy," he replied, annoyed.

"Doesn't it feel boring to be alone in this dungeon?" I said sarcastically. But this idiotic guy took it seriously.

"Yeah, but what choice do I have? It happens to the best of us," he said, sounding a little sad. But he cleared his throat, saying, "Okay enough with these games, let me finish you!"

He almost landed a punch on me, but Ryan suddenly threw a stone at him. It did not hurt him at all. He turned towards Ryan angrily. I knew the only way to kill this guy was to throw a stick of TNT into his mouth; his body could not bear heat for a long time. I mouthed the word 'TNT' to Ryan, and I assumed he understood.

"I will kill you first and then the kid," the man was telling Ryan.

"You are such a weak person that you need to kill me in your human form, eh mate?" Ryan said.

"I thought you wanted a fair fight," the dragon replied.

"Yes, I do -- so transform into a dragon and fight me with all your power," Ryan said arrogantly.

The man was angry and transformed into a dragon again. I knew Ryan understood the plan. The dragon's throat was burning with all the heat. Suddenly, I noticed Aaliyah and James climb in through a secret tunnel on the far end of the dungeon.

I grabbed the two backpacks filled with gold. I grabbed Stephan, who was injured, and made my way to Aaliyah and James. We were waiting for Ryan to show up after throwing dynamite into the dragon's mouth. Stephan and my friends had no idea what Ryan was trying to do, so I explained it to them. We were scared but excited to see what would happen.

The dragon opened its mouth, but before it could breathe out fire, Ryan threw the dynamite into its mouth. The dragon began choking on it and looked like it couldn't breathe.

Ryan ran up to us and told us to leave. "What! Not without you," Stephan said.

"That TNT can destroy the whole mine and kill all of you! Someone has to control the explosion," Ryan said.

"How are you going to do it," I asked.

"My powers will let me absorb all the energy, but it will kill me," he replied.

"No, that's not going to happen. Either we all survive, or we all die," Stephan said.

Ryan looked at all of us and gave me a smile. He nodded us farewell and pushed us towards the tunnel leading out of the cave. As we were leaving, I saw him press the detonator. We heard a huge explosion, which abruptly stopped. We knew he had contained it.

He died like a hero and had wanted this for a long time. It was his plan to sacrifice himself in the mine.

"He was my brother. I loved him more than anything," Stephan said and wiped his tears. I expected Stephan to break down, but this guy was apparently emotionless.

James noticed the gold and was the happiest man alive.

"Holy shit we did it!" Aaliyah said.

"What now?" I asked Stephan.

"Well, we leave this cave and head back to a safe place. We definitely can't enter the hotel with all this gold," he said.

When we walked out of the cave, we were still in the mines. We could see the cave that we first went through, and the wooden blocks were still guarding it. If Ryan had not been there, the whole mine would be in pieces. We managed to get to the Mokottam cliffs. We drove for an hour and stopped at a small house. An old man welcomed us and hugged Stephan. "Kids, meet my close friend, Christopher. He is a doctor and can treat us," Stephan said.

We were all pretty banged-up and needed multiple stitches. Christopher gave us anaesthesia and treated us. We woke up after a few hours and I quickly checked to see if the gold was still there. The doctor entered the room.

"Don't worry, I won't steal the treasure. I would never betray

Stephan after what he has done for me," he said.

I noticed my friends and Stephan were awake too. "Well, now we have the gold. What do we do," I asked.

"We can sell it and get back home," Aaliyah said.

"It isn't that easy, sweetie," Christopher said with a smile.

"We have fifty bars of gold that was originally going to be split between the four of us. But we would all be dead if not for Christopher, so he is part of the deal too. He gets ten bars. I have booked a flight back to Canada for this evening. We go to the airport and get caught on purpose during the security check. Every police agency in the world is looking for us. They will interrogate us, and you guys must pretend to be innocent and know nothing about any treasure. I will surrender on charges of kidnapping three children and getting involved with mafias around the world. We don't mention the treasure at all. All the evidence points only to me and you guys can get away scot-free. You will be sent back to Canada and pretend like nothing happened. Christopher will sell the gold in Cairo and send you the money. You get my share as well – I won't need it in jail," Stephan said and sighed.

"Wait, no. That's not happening, there's no way you are turning yourself in. You can manage the police, right?" I asked.

"Well, I could do that, but I have committed many crimes in my life and it's time to pay up," Stephan said.

I was extremely sad upon hearing this, but this was the only way me and my friends could live freely. I really wanted to see my family and hug them, so I had no option but to listen to Stephan.

"Wait, so fifty divided by four gives us 12.5 bars of gold -- which is how many Canadian dollars?" Aaliyah asked.

"One bar weighs one kilo, and 12.5 bars of gold is worth over a million dollars," Christopher replied.

"Holy crap! We are going to be rich," James said.

"That's not all -- this gold is incredibly rare, so bidders will pay much more than you think," Christopher said.

Stephan smiled and closed his eyes. I knew this Christopher guy was more than just a doctor. We got ready as it was almost time for our flight. We decided to leave early so that we could execute our plan. We left the gold with Christopher and got into the two cars waiting outside. Of course, one was a Ferrari and the other a Maserati. I looked at Stephan and he nodded.

I got into the driver seat of the Ferrari with Aaliyah. This was like a dream come true. I followed Stephan's car -- it was a pretty long drive. I was enjoying every minute of it. I had driving lessons back in Vancouver, but I never had a car for myself. I was having the time of my life until we reached the airport. We were probably the only people in the world to leave a sports car at an airport with no intention of returning.

Stephan informed me to leave the key near the car so that some poor soul may take it. I never knew Stephan was so generous, but it was a pleasant surprise. We didn't have any luggage. Before we entered the airport, we grabbed coffee and a quick bite near the airport.

"Well, I guess this is it," Stephan said.

"But we will see you again, right?" I asked.

"I meant this is the last time that we mention the treasure. We do not want anyone to lay hands on something so precious. What did you think I was talking about," Stephan said with a wink.

Aaliyah and James nodded. We went inside the airport. Luckily, the three of us had kept our passports safely. When we went through security and they checked our documents, an alarm rang throughout the airport. All the officers there rushed forward and arrested us. We were treated harshly, but we did commit a lot of crimes.

IT ALL COMES TOGETHER

Chapter 13

About thirty security officers had their guns pointed at us. We were surrounded on all sides and had to lay down on the floor with our hands up. We were escorted out of the airport, where the real police officers were waiting for us. We were put in separate police vehicles for some reason and were driven to the police station in Cairo.

The police captain was waiting for us at the station. He did not say anything to us and threw us into the interrogation room. We were all in separate rooms and could not see each other. I waited in my chair for a while until the captain came in. He kept asking me questions, but Stephan had told me not to say anything and to strictly not demand a lawyer.

"So, Leo Schmidt, you have the perfect parents and even a house in Vancouver -- but one day you suddenly decided to leave home and commit federal crimes in multiple countries including Canada, Brazil, Belarus and even Germany," he said and slammed his hand against the table.

I followed Stephan's instructions to blame everything on him. "No sir, Stephan kidnapped us and forced us to commit these crimes. He told us that he would kill our parents," I said.

"And why did he choose you out of all the millions of kids out there in the world, huh?" the captain said.

"Ask him yourself," I replied.

The captain questioned me for a long time, and I was certain he did not believe my story. He suspected something bigger was at stake. He kept asking me questions, but I refused to co-operate. He slammed his hand on the table and walked out of the room. A bulky-looking officer came in and threw me in the lockup. It was in the worst condition possible, but at least my friends and Stephan were there too. We had to speak softly and make sure the officers didn't hear anything.

"The cops aren't buying the story, but the German and Canadian police will soon be here. I will confess to all the crimes and looking at the evidence, they will be certain that I did everything and will believe our story," Stephan said in a soft voice.

"Won't we have to go to the court?" Aaliyah asked.

"Not at all. I will confess my crimes to the police. I will be arrested and put into solitary confinement, and I will be taken to the court. It will probably be a life sentence," Stephan said.

"Whatever happens, all we can do now is wait," James said.

We were brought out of the lockup after a long six hours. The FBI and CIA were there too -- this had become much bigger than I expected. They handcuffed Stephan and pushed him away from us.

"We have a warrant to arrest you. You're going down for your crimes and kidnapping these young men and woman," an FBI officer said.

Stephan did not say anything and co-operated with them. As he was being escorted out of the police station, he winked at us. I had no idea where he went, but I was sure he was going to have a tough time there. The officers said they were sorry for what we went through. I knew they bought the story, but I was scared for Stephan and what they were going to do to him. My friends and I were escorted out of the station and the CIA got in touch with our parents.

We were sent back to Vancouver with a government official because we were still wanted there. When we landed, we were greeted by our parents at the airport. Aaliyah's mother hugged her and started crying. James's father was sober for once and apologised to his son for his drinking. They hugged too.

I ran up to my parents and hugged them tightly. We headed back home. I was happy to see James happy with his father as they went to their place.

The next day, the CIA and FBI's statement was in the newspaper. It said, "Stephan Kaiser, the wanted criminal, has been arrested and awarded life imprisonment for a string of crimes including murder, arson, and kidnapping three teenagers." I knew this was bullshit, but was what Stephan wanted. My parents and the whole world completely bought the story.

I was grounded for the next three months. I had a lot of time to think about everything that happened. I knew that Jake, the guy we saw in Rio, helped Stephan erase the evidence of me and my friends killing our attackers. But I still wondered why Stephan turned himself in. College was completely crap after that. Everyone knew that we were the kids who were kidnapped, and even though our names weren't released to the public, we did vanish for two months without a trace. It didn't feel like two months, but I guess time flies.

The days went by in a blur, and we had forgotten all about the gold, until one day. My parents and I were sitting in the hall, casually talking, until she brought something up.

"Leo are you ever going to tell us what happened in those two months?" she asked.

But before I could say anything, a notification popped up on my father's phone that made him jump out of his seat. He had suddenly received a payment of one million dollars from an unknown account. I pretended to know nothing about this and ran to my room. I called my friends, and they told me that they received the money too.

It was sent by Christopher. He must have sold the gold in Cairo. I assumed he had taken the money all for himself, because we had not received word of it for a while, but he turned out to be a good person.

I couldn't believe that I had all this money now. I could do anything I wanted! I bought a Ferrari Roma, which I loved, after I got my driving license. Life was going great until I started missing the adventures with Stephan. I decided to head to Malrow's Café by myself, just to sip that wonderful coffee and cherish the memory of when it all started. I especially loved the coffee there, but I could never afford it before all this. I ordered a cappuccino and sipped it slowly.

I was getting late for a class, and I definitely couldn't afford to miss any more. I asked the waiter for the bill, and he told me that it was already taken care of. When I asked who paid for the coffee, he pointed me towards a man reading a newspaper. I looked at him, and he slowly put down his newspaper. It was Stephan sipping his coffee. He put on his shades and nodded at me, smiling.

Stephan had planned all this before, from the very beginning. He was never in it for the gold – he wanted to connect with his family's heritage. How he managed to get himself out of all this was a mystery by itself.

*

1865

Mary Thompson, direct descendant of one of the crew members manages to find the treasure but dies in the hands of the treasure god.

1613

Fredrick Silverhand and his crew begin the hunt for the lost Drakon mines.

1930

Jacob Weiser along with Julia Fraser stumble upon a map which was drawn by Mary Thompson. They manage to get to Atacama Desert but only Julia survives.

2001

Ryan and Stephan realise about the treasure and manage to find the initial two locations but never end up reaching both due to unforeseen circumstances which causes Ryan's death.

2016

Leo realises his grandfather Jacob Weiser managed to almost get to the treasure but died. He decides to complete this journey with his friends and Stephan finds out about this and seeks his help.

ACKNOWLEDGEMENTS

Adithi N is a visual communication and branding designer (graphic designer in simpler terms) who works with motivated brands by helping them build bold stories and emotional connections.

Aditi Kumar is an editor and writer with an MA in Publishing from the University of Exeter. A former journalist, she is an avid reader and a fan of all things literary.

ABOUT THE AUTHOR

Vedanth .S. Reddy, from Bengaluru. Having just completed his 10th in Sishu Griha senior school. He is currently sixteen years of age. At the age of eleven he published his first book "The legacy of Phoenix". Vedanth enjoys reading books and watching movies.

You can write to me at vedanth0811@gmail.com

www.ingramcontent.com/pod-product-compliance
Lightning Source LLC
LaVergne TN
LVHW041127150826
845673LV00007B/2211

* 9 7 9 8 8 9 6 3 2 5 4 6 8 *